# A Suitable Demise

**By**

**Andrew Clark**

First Published in 2022 by Blossom Spring Publishing
A Suitable Demise Copyright © 2022 Andrew Clark
ISBN 978-1-7398866-1-5
E: admin@blossomspringpublishing.com
W: www.blossomspringpublishing.com
Published in the United Kingdom.

## About The Author

Andrew Clark lives and works in rural North Yorkshire. He has a life-long connection to the county, although his family hails from the west of Scotland. His early career was in nursing as a Registered General Nurse and after 7 years nursing, he joined the Police Service in which he had a successful career specialising in covert policing. Now retired, he works in a local independent bookshop.

Andrew enjoys walking with his family and dogs, has a passion for books, art and playing musical instruments. His inspiration to write comes from his experiences in nursing and policing and his gained insights into human nature. His crime fiction offers an honest and unique insight based on personal experience.

I dedicate this book to my family.

# Chapter 1

## January 2016

Rain drove relentlessly, whipped by a frenzied wind, into the face of PC Jason Perry, who stood at the gates of 119. It was 3 am and he'd been given the unenviable job of protecting the outer cordon of the crime scene. A dry, warm marked police vehicle stood parked and empty ten yards away from him, its presence calling to him, the keys in his pocket.

"No, don't do it Jase," he mumbled to himself, "I'm bloody freezing, soaked, forty-six years old, being battered by the sea's finest punches but if I get in that car, I'll have my backside handed to me on a plate by the job."

Perry looked behind him to see young PC Owens smile and wave, standing within the covered porch of the front door, clipboard in hand. Perry responded with a two fingered wave, turned back to the sea and raised his fluorescent coat collar against the elements. His first ten minutes at the scene had passed. Only four more hours to go until the early turn would take over.

Overlooking the North Sea on the cliffs to the south side of Barnston, 119 Palmerston View stood resolute. The second floor windows enjoyed a terrific view of the harbour, which rose steeply north and west towards limestone cliffs. The Victorian detached house stood within large gardens surrounded by neat laurel hedges. A block stone drive with an electric black wrought iron gate and intercom entry, snaked to the front door. The house spoke of money and the venetian blue Jaguar F-type sat upon the driveway reflected this.

The owner, Mr Frank Wellbury, also owned retail premises within the town and was well-known in the community. He had grown up in Barnston, attended local schools and colleges and made a "success" of his life. A self-made man, at forty-five years old, he was still the town's renowned bachelor, whose private affairs few knew of but many contemplated. Wellbury was an astute businessman whose public face smiled but he tolerated no fools. At six foot tall and weighing twenty-four stones, although formidable, his pallid complexion spoke of health issues. Lights on at the house, Wellbury was at home.

On either side of the gate, the premises' hedge had a blue and white tape with 'Police' emblazoned thereon, therefore acting as a deterrent to everyone. Raised crime scene steps now provided a path to the front door. Crime Scene Investigation were present and had taken control of the scene. The press hadn't landed – yet!

\*\*\*

Rachel stirred to the tones of Sheeran's 'Castle on the Hill' as it gently pulled her from her sleep. She reached over to her mobile and squinted at the phone. 3 am and a blocked number: *must be work.*

"Hello."

"Sergeant Barnes, control room. Sorry to wake you, but I'm calling you out, Sarge. There's a car on the way. It'll be there in ten and you'll be briefed at the scene."

"OK, no problem," mumbled Rachel. The phone went dead. *Bloody hell*, thought Rachel. She looked over to Matthew beside her, who smiled and turned over.

"Take care and keep safe," he mumbled, giving her a desultory thumbs up.

Rachel exited the bed, grabbed some clothes and went to the bathroom to change. Trousers and shirt on, eyeliner complete, she went downstairs to the kitchen and put the kettle on. Dishes still adorned the work surfaces from last night's dinner. A couple of wine glasses held the red dregs of the corner shop's best, and still half a bottle left. *Thank goodness I only had one glass*, she thought. Rachel made a coffee and looking out of her front window, watched the two bright lights of a marked police vehicle pull up outside her address. She grabbed her coat and coffee and exiting the front door, was greeted by the torrential rain. Shutting the door, she ran to the vehicle, jumping in the back.

"Hi guys, what have we got?" she asked.

"Hi Sarge, we've to drive you to the scene at Palmerston View. We've been told nothing else. Jones is in charge, so good luck there."

Rachel arrived outside 119, having been driven across town.

"Cheers," she said and getting out of the car, noted that the scene was fully locked down.

"Hi Jase, drawn the short straw?"

"Bloody right I have, Acting Inspector Barnes." Rachel had been given a temporary promotion two weeks ago to head the CID department. Jase had to shout, "Out in this relentless storm whilst young Owens up there, dry as a bone. You'd better get in there. Steps are out and the boss is waiting for you." Rachel looked at the house. This is an important one, she thought.

Ensuring that she used the CSI steps, placed to protect the area, Rachel approached the front door, where Owens signed her in as attending the scene. His role was to record all persons entering and exiting the house to ensure that CSI could eliminate police officer marks and traces from the scene at a later date, should it be required. Rachel entered the hallway of the house and was confronted by a corridor with stairs to the left, presumably leading to the second floor. Four doors led from the corridor, all open, and CSI officers in their white suits were working industriously.

"In here, Barnes," said the stern and cigarette roughened voice of Detective Superintendent Jones. Rachel entered the room first on the right, hands in pockets, and walked into a lavish home office. Within the office were Jones, a CSI and Mr Frank Wellbury. Indeed, Wellbury was at home. At home and as dead as a doornail!

Rachel quickly scanned the scene. Wellbury sat in a green leather and wooden office chair behind a tidy walnut desk. Wearing a grey T-shirt, his arms resting upon the chair arms, with eyes closed, head forward, his face and lips cyanosed, his neck appeared bloated and skin pallid. Dark coloured material was protruding from his mouth and rested upon his shirt, a pool of saliva spreading where it touched, staining the material. The office was tidy with no signs of any search or struggle. Windows appeared secure and undamaged, as did the door. Wellbury looked 'settled'. It all looked wrong.

"Over here, Rachel" said Jones, pointing to the floor to the left of Wellbury. On the carpeted floor lay burnt tinfoil, a lighter and a 'tooting' tube.

"Heroin?" said Rachel, recognising the items for 'chasing the dragon' (lighter placed under the foil heating the heroin and the tube used to inhale the fumes which spiralled from the drug).

"This doesn't look right, Boss," said Rachel.

"Bloody right it doesn't, Inspector. I've been here thirty minutes, CSI forty minutes. Golden hour, Rachel. Golden hour for us to capture best evidence. You've got two detectives outside and a couple of uniform. CSI has the house and uniform's got the cordon secure. You've seen the scene. Brief your staff and get them working; start by securing what evidence you can. You know what to do. We're treating this as a murder scene so get all the staff we need; full briefing at ten this morning. I'm off to brief the Chief. The bloody press are going to be all over this." With that, Jones marched from the room, leaving Rachel in his wake.

\*\*\*

At six thirty, Matthew opened his eyes as the Fitbit on his wrist gently vibrated, rousing him from sleep. He stretched and climbed out of bed, slipped some shorts and a shirt on and nipped to the loo. Electric toothbrush in hand, he looked at himself in the mirror as he brushed. At forty years old he was still lean and felt in his prime. A dark mop of curly hair capped his six foot frame and a dark beard hid his 'boyish' looks. Deep brown eyes looked back at him, reflecting a hidden intellect behind a calm face. He spat and smiled, examining his teeth. Satisfied, he recapped the paste, rinsed his brush and switched off the light. Duvet straight, Matthew was ready for his morning run.

In the kitchen, last night's takeaway dishes remained unwashed and the kettle stood on the counter, off its stand. Matthew replaced it and decided the dishes could wait until he got back. The rest of the house was tidy; he could sort the kitchen in a jiffy. Matthew struggled with mess, Rachel didn't. Rachel didn't allow mess to dominate her consciousness whereas, though obviously not OCD, Matthew needed it tidy. He put on his running jacket, pushed his hair back and stuck on a cap backwards. Stepping out of the door, the rain from last night had ceased and a grey dawn encroached upon the horizon. The salty air smelt clean and sharp as Matthew jogged out of his driveway, heading for the sea cliffs above the North Bay.

Matthew loved the peacefulness of running. He never played music, just allowed his mind to wander and enjoy the beauty of the run. He climbed the gently rising road and crossed over the coast road towards the cliffs. Running into the wind, his pace was steady as he ran at the side of a ploughed field and hit the coastal path. He stopped, looking out to sea, watching seagulls wheeling in the sky or tracking fishing trawlers as they navigated their routes home. The sea looked wild, its white capped rollers smashing into a pebbled beach, cleansing its soul. Matthew felt alive, the wind propping him as he leaned forwards, trusting to its arbitrary embrace. Standing at the cliff edge, a sheer drop, he relished the danger, despite the cliff hazard signs which were clearly displayed. *What if?* he thought, leaning forward. The wind skipped a heartbeat and Matthew with it as he quickly jerked back.

"NOT TODAY!" he shouted, his eyes wild. He laughed, turned left and continued running his five-mile morning route. The cliff route took him North towards the old disused railway line which tracked back towards his house. The line was protected from the gusting wind, so Matthew increased his pace for the last stretch, relishing his feeling of fitness. He'd not brought his phone and idiotically had forgotten to text Rachel before he left the house to check that she was OK. Full pace, down the road towards the house now, then he walked it off; Matthew arrived back at home.

Opening the door, he heard the familiar 'ping' of a text. Checking his phone, it was Rachel.

*Hi Matt, I'm afraid it's going to be a long day. I'll be home late. Not sure when. I'll let you know when I do … xxx*

*OK love. Keep safe x,* replied Matthew.

He couldn't complain. He was late last night, rescuing himself only by bringing back a takeaway and a bottle of red. Both of them were used to their transient lifestyle, though if truth be told, Matthew felt that he regularly drew the short straw, spending many evenings on his own. *Oh well*, he thought.

He stripped off, jumped in the shower and dressed in a collared shirt, chinos and brown brogues. Downstairs in the kitchen, the takeaway boxes were placed in the bin (outside), dishes in the dishwasher and surfaces cleaned with Morrison's kitchen cleaner (with bleach). Looking back at the kitchen he smiled, you wouldn't know anything had been there. It was immaculate.

Stepping outside, Matthew placed on his Barbour greatcoat and checked his phone. No more messages. Now only eight thirty, he decided to catch the bus into town for work. He had the time. A walk along the road past the tennis courts and he could catch the 9A to town and work. He checked his phone again - Settings, account, find my iPhone and switched it on. All was good with the world. Matthew smiled and strode off in the direction of the bus stop.

\*\*\*

Rachel walked up to the back entrance of Barnston Police Station, which was situated within the town, its red brickwork matching that of the local Magistrates Court adjoining, both depicting an air of solidity and partnership for law and order. Rachel used her warrant card, placed it against the smart lock and entered the rear yard of the police station.

Her senses were assaulted, an enormous cannabis mother plant floated past her towards the drug store supported by a pair of blue gloved hands. A task force van sat within the compound, loaded with lights, fans, drainage pipes and evidence bags, clearly seized from a large cannabis grow. The task force (TF) were lounging around the van, watching a couple of young probationers unloading, joking with each other and 'managing' the seizure. One cop smoked a fag, which was quickly docked and dropped under a black booted heel. Another gigantic male standing and, as far as Rachel could see, flexing his muscles in a show of male vanity and clear desperation. Rachel looked at his face. *Good looking lad, but nowt else in there*, she thought.

Jane Scriven came walking from the store. She was the team's skipper and had her hands full with this lot. The testosterone scale within this team was high and she'd been brought in as a strong manager in order to 'increase professionalism' within the unit.

"Right, get this all shifted into the store," she said to all of them. Although sluggish, there was a response.

"We are straight on to another search at Palmerston," she clarified.

"Morning, Rach, long night? We're off to your scene as soon as I'm finished here. CSI is still there but we'll start the fingertip search in the rooms they've completed. I've got the search parameters and will let you know if there's anything significant."

"Cheers, Jane. I'm tired already but it's going to be a longer day. The press are up there already so good luck getting past them," replied Rachel.

"They'll not bother us. I'll just send Hulk Hogan out of the van first," she replied, nodding towards the team's man mountain. "No one will be able to see past him and the best they'll get in a reply is a grunt," she whispered quietly.

Rachel smiled as she entered the building and headed towards CID to check in and dump her stuff prior to the 10 am briefing. The office was quiet with just a couple of detectives working on computers at their desks. Neither looked up, probably working through the technical wizardry of electronic witness statements as they hurdled through the complexity of case file preparation. Other desks were empty with varying degrees of mess and tidiness, neither of which indicated the ability or not of an officer. An aroma of stale fish'n'chips loitered in the air and worn, stained, carpet tiles patterned the floor. The office was tired and in desperate need of a full refurbishment. Rachel had her own small office, in no better shape, adjacent to the main office, in which a cluttered desk had a fetching view of a marigold-coloured painted wall with a smattering of hairline cracks crawling towards the ceiling. She grabbed her blue day diary and green Major Incident Book and stepped out of the office, turned left and walked the short corridor to the ladies' loo. Unsurprisingly, the estate management plan had placed the DI's office next to the men's toilet, to the amusement of many officers and civilians in the nick. Even within her two weeks, Acting Inspector Rachel could tell that Ronnie Cuthbertson had eaten the incandescent curry and partaken of the Crown and Cushion's Guinness, following the usual Wednesday night piss-up.

Rachel placed her books next to the sink and checked herself. At forty-two years old, Rachel was still reasonably trim and although middle age spread was encroaching, she was determined to hold it at bay. Her chestnut hair was in disarray after the squalls of the night, so she straightened it with the tangle brush retrieved from her shoulder bag. Eyeliner remained in place; with a naturally freckled face and soft complexion, she never used other make up as a rule. She looked tired though and hated to think how she'd look later in the day. Rachel nipped for a pee, straightened her shirt and trousers and was ready to face the throng, in what would be her first serious case as a Deputy Senior Investigative Officer or Deputy SIO.

The briefing room was on the top floor of the station. Rachel climbed the internal stairs, not trusting the reliability of the aging interior lift. There was a buzz in the air, as she reached the top floor, of people's voices, with the excitement of a murder investigation in its infancy. The thrill of a whodunit! Every officer would play an integral part in investigating, identifying and arresting the offender. Murder was uncommon in Barnston and any officer worth her or his salt wanted to be part of this. D/Supt Jones had an office next to the briefing room and Rachel knocked, waited for "Come in" and entered.

Jones sat behind a desk which had a computer on it. He was a large imposing man with a stern face. Old school, he was not a bloke to get on the wrong side of. Grey suited, white shirt with a Windsor knot tied perfectly, he had high standards and expected others to have them too. His newly issued policy book sat on the desk, the first pages already full with his script. This would be the book in which he would record all his thoughts, decision making processes, justification for action and hypothesis as the investigation developed. Another knock at the door and Detective Inspector Andy Burrows walked in.

"Morning sir," said Andy with a soft Scottish accent, "Rachel," he smiled, shaking her hand.

"Right," said Jones. "The Senior Management Team gathered. It's great to have you both. Obviously, I'm the SIO, Rachel Dep. and Senior Investigator; Andy will manage the intelligence cell. I've got a Sergeant looking after the computerised case file and compiling and collating all the actions. All decisions will go through us; I'll script them up. I don't know all of the answers and it's the team's job to find them. This is going to be high profile and the press are all over it. I'll deal with them with the force press officer. We keep everything tight and the team does too. The Chief Officer team is watching and I don't want my arse kicked by them."

"Sir," replied Rachel and Andy in unison.

"Right, out there to the room and get them ready. I'll be in there in two."

Rachel and Andy turned to the door, Andy reaching for the handle.

"Guys," advised Jones, "in here it's Bob. Out there, Sir or Boss is fine."

Both smiled and exited, walking towards the briefing room and entered the fray. There were a number of chairs encircling the room with three free chairs at the head of the circle. All other chairs were occupied with the dedicated investigation team being a mix of all sorts. Rachel recognised most, as they had spent their careers at Barnston, with just a couple of fresh young faces new to her. She looked at Andy and took the lead.

"Right, everyone," she said, in a slightly raised voice, "the boss will be here in two minutes to start the briefing. He'll expect your full attention. Everyone got their green books?" Mumbled assents of affirmation. "All notes to go in there and nowhere else. Ronnie's got disclosure for the case." Ronnie Cuthbertson raised his hand in acknowledgement with a slight grimace as the team gently laughed. Disclosure in a case was a tedious but essential job. Ronnie's role would be to collate all material gained by all the officers during the case and schedule it as necessary. This would then allow him to ascertain its relevance to the investigation and enable him to provide the prosecution and defence attorneys with all the material that they would require to prosecute or defend the offender. Rachel smiled, raising her hands for quiet.

"I know, I know, but I have to get some recompense for Ronnie's Thursday morning trips to the gents!" A gentle laughter from the team in response.

The door then opened and in walked Jones. Chairs scraped back on dark blue squared floor tiles as older officers, who still remembered historically enforced rules, showed their respect for rank and stood up. A good many personnel, police staff and police officers, remained seated, not believing or recognising the need to stand. Jones surveyed the room, expressionless, and sat down. The standing officers sat also.

"Morning everyone," said Jones in his broad Yorkshire accent. The room went silent.

"At 1 am this morning a telephone call was made to the Force Control Room by an unknown person. The number was withheld, the caller advised the control room that they should send a police officer to 119 Palmerston View. The call was then terminated. The voice was muffled, calm and sounded like a male. No other information was provided. At 3 am this morning I arrived at 119 Palmerston View, the home address of Mr Frank Wellbury, the victim. Wellbury was sitting within his study and clearly had been dead for some time. Having attended the scene, I am satisfied that the circumstances are suspicious and therefore at this time have declared this a murder investigation." Jones looked around the room at each officer, ensuring that he had their full attention. "Rachel, Andy and I will lead the investigation. I know you may already know each other but can we go around the room from my left, introduce yourself and tell everyone your role in the investigation?" The round started with declarations of CSI, exhibits officer, financial investigator, enquiry team, analyst and a raft of roles required for the enquiry, rolling out from members of the team.

"Right," said Jones. "Ground rules. Everything said within this room stays within the room. You have my full trust and I wish to keep it that way. Any person speaking inappropriately outside of this room will immediately be taken off the enquiry. All persons working will either be in uniform or suited and booted as appropriate. We are and will remain a professional unit at all times." Jones smiled, although this did not appear to be conveyed through his eyes. "Every person's thoughts, opinions, guesswork, within this team, are of value to the enquiry so don't be afraid to shout up. I will not be able to solve this crime alone and it will be one of you, who innocuously mentions something within our briefings that breaks the case." He paused, again looking around the room. "Right, many of you know the ropes. I'll write all the policies which will drive all the actions that we undertake. The result of your actions will inform my policy as we investigate and make headway. With that, I want Colin, our Crime Scene Investigator, to take us through the scene." He nodded to the CSI and Colin remotely switched on the smart board at the end of the room, displaying a photograph of 119 Palmerston as he commenced.

"......... so in summary," continued Colin, "No forced entry to the house that we can find. The study itself seems tidy and Wellbury appeared to be an organised man with everything in its place. An initial quick look around the room revealed a corner where carpet was clearly pulled away from the gripper and underneath disclosed a floor safe, still closed. Wellbury sat at his desk in comfortable clothing. On the floor next to him, foil with drug traces thereon, and a lighter. The top right desk drawer was slightly open and further examination revealed a cellophane wrap containing five foiled wraps of brown powder. Field testing indicates heroin. Finally, protruding from his mouth was dark red material, which I've left in place for the pathologist to remove. I've looked at it closely and I could be wrong but it looks like the top end of a sock!" Colin zoomed in on the facial image of Wellbury highlighting the material and sat down. The room was silent and then murmurs started.

"So," started Jones, "a well-known individual, possible heroin user, who appears to be ingesting material similar to socks and no forced entry. Nothing is known about his drug misuse and nothing to indicate any problems in his life. It's now our job to discover what happened and why."

During the next hour, Jones went around the room and listened to opinions. Rachel allocated tasks to each person and Andy advised the team of his requirements for the intelligence cell.

Bringing the briefing to a close, Jones stated, "I have been involved in a number of investigations and when I was a young cop was told the following by an experienced detective. Work by A, B, C and you won't go wrong. Accept nothing, believe nobody, check everything. That's what I want from you ladies and gents, A, B, C. Give me your best." With that, Jones stood up and walked out of the room.

# Chapter 2

Matthew jumped off the 9A at the top of town, saying thanks to the driver and commenced his walk through the streets towards his rented shop. The once magnificent Victorian railway station, at the top of the town, stood imperiously looking over the precinct, its clock face tower chiming nine thirty. A stiff breeze swept the streets making passers-by huddle conspiratorially into their raincoats, holding hats down, hiding their faces. Matthew strode down the centre, head held high with hair whipping about his face.

"What a great day to be alive," he said to himself, as he walked beyond banks and shop doors closed against the elements. Stopping at a newsagent, a headline blared at him,

'Local businessman found dead!'

Matthew immediately thought of Rachel, her call in the night and her turning out for work. *Well, she'll call me later or I'll see her later on tonight,* he thought.

Continuing on, the regular Big Issue seller in the town stood, magazine in hand, with a drawn face divulging his addiction to those in the know. Matthew headed to him with his change and took a copy.

"OK, Matt? Cheers," said the male gratefully in a West Yorkshire accent, as Matthew bought a copy. Matthew nodded and moved on with his magazine, which he unceremoniously dumped in a bin one hundred yards on. The Big Issue seller wouldn't care. He had another £2.50 towards his takings.

He headed towards his shop on one of the side streets and opened the door to Forseti's Bookshop. Entering, the alarm began to sound as Matthew went to the control panel and entered the numeric code required to silence it. The shop, although a modern store, had the customary aroma of books and the settled air of an oasis offering an unbridled tranquillity to book browsers and purchasers alike. Matthew went to the sales counter, switching on the Epos till, listening to familiar sounds as it kicked into life. He switched on the store lights and stood proudly looking round the shop which catered for all manner of book lovers. All sections were neat as he had left it last night, with book spines clearly visible and sales tables neat and tidy. A Chesterfield chair, in wine red leather, stood invitingly in one corner at the rear of the shop next to an electric log burner, a mantlepiece and parlour palm, enticing readers to rest a while in the business of their day. He was proud of his shop, which made a modest profit and, happy things were tidy, he opened the front door, welcoming any person walking past. Matthew had built up some loyal regulars, who would visit to peruse new stock and to buy the best sellers and books to be discussed at the next book club meeting. He was also known to be Rachel's partner, Barnston being a small town, which had its benefits of discouraging the minor criminal element from shopping, or indeed shoplifting, within the shop. He stuck the kettle on in the rear kitchen, made a coffee and re-entered the store area.

Entering the shop was a local 'don' Geoff, whose glasses had steamed up from the effects of the collision of cold and warm air. He shuffled to the rear of the store and began examining the crime thriller section. In five minutes, he would probably be sitting in the Chesterfield chair enjoying the ambience. Within the doorway stood Joe, boyhood friend of Matthew, renowned shoplifter and heroin addict. Matthew beckoned him in and passed him his own freshly made coffee.

"Cheers, mate," Joe said, as he sipped from the hot cup. "Have you seen the bloody headlines?"

"Language, Joe, please," Matthew replied, raising his

eyebrows, "Yes, do you know who it is?" he asked.

"Sorry mate," Joe shrugged his shoulders apologetically for his language, "only bloody Fat Wellbury. Can you believe it?" covering his mouth with his hand and then mouthing, "Sorry," again silently.

"Wellbury, eh!" replied Matthew.

"Yep, he was a bloomin' smackhead, you know," whispered Joe conspiratorially, "Liked to toot it he did, never injected, been using it for yonks. We bloody knew. Probably overdosed on the bloody stuff. What an idiot!" said Joe in his staccato phraseology. "Do you remember him at college? He was always better than the rest of us; picked on a few, pissed off a few and always guaranteed to get a job in the family business. Some things just come easy to some. Well, maybe he deserved this too. Who knows? Poor sod." With that, Joe handed the coffee back and sauntered from the shop, warm and ready to start his day job – shoplifting!

*Fatty Wellbury*, Matthew thought to himself, *a heroin addict and now dead?*

Joe's group of friends now circled around heroin supply and purchase. Matthew had known him for years; he had gone through school and college with him. He was an intelligent lad who could have done well if he hadn't succumbed to the addiction of heroin. Wellbury he'd known too. Always a bit of a smart arse who had scraped through school and college, always knowing that he'd be employed by his parents when he finished. He was a big lad who was happy to throw his weight about physically and verbally, especially when he took the reins over at the family shops. Matthew had heard that he'd pissed off a few employees and wasn't liked by many.

As Joe had been chatting, Richard Greaves had entered the shop and was quietly looking around adult fiction. Another man who had grown up in Barnston and in the distant past had been bullied by Wellbury. Greaves was a small man of skinny build who looked fragile. Wrapped up in a thick parka against the elements and wearing some round wired glasses he resembled a mole, his thinning close cropped hair completing the look. He rarely spoke to Matthew, just nodding to him and giving him a weak smile as a greeting. Matthew had no idea what he did for a living now but had heard that he had a small flat in the town centre. He shrugged his shoulders and checked his stock management system. The system logged all books bought and sold and held a database of customers, as well as allowing Matthew to deal with invoices, returns and also enabled him to search for titles required by customers. January was always a quiet time in the shop, following the Christmas rush, so Matthew did some quick housekeeping before he would get the opportunity to sit down and read. Reading was his greatest passion which his small business allowed him to indulge in when quiet. Finishing his computer work, he sat down at the counter and buried his head into Leo Tolstoy's "Anna Karenina" as the day passed him by.

\*\*\*

Joe raised the hood on his Rockport coat and wandered into the precinct. Despite the cold weather, he was sweating, his hands were shaking and his stomach cramping: the crap feelings of addiction with his body telling him he needed a fix. He was skint and his giro wasn't due for two days so petty crime would have to get him his tenner for a wrap. The town was getting busier and it would be easier to steal with more people around, as they'd provide better cover for him. He'd head to Tesco's and nick some booze which was easy to flog on. First though to find which 'line' was on. Approaching the

Big Issue seller, it was a quick "Now then," a handshake and a small slip of paper passed into Joe's hand. Looking at the slip it had Tommy 07959828764 written on it. So, the Scousers were back in town.

Barnston's Class A supply was controlled by the Northern cities and larger towns who sent young teenagers (kids) to the coast to sell their drugs. The kids would be dropped off or travel by train to the town where they would seek out a vulnerable drug user and tell them they were staying at their flat, using violence to enforce this message, if it was required. The flat was then used as a base for their drug supply for a while, until they moved on to another vulnerable person. A system referred to in the papers as 'cuckooing'. 'Cuckooing' – the practice of taking over the home of a vulnerable person in order to establish a base for illegal drug dealing, typically part of a County Lines operation.

County Lines drug supply was the scourge of coastal towns and drove the supply and demand. Both teenage suppliers and local users stuck in a never ending spiralling circle. The teenage suppliers were recruited at an early age and forced to deal in towns like Barnston under personal threat, or threat to family 'back home' if they refused to do so. Local users who have chosen, in the eyes of the general public, 'the wrong path in life', whose addiction drove their daily decisions and who were subject to violence over drug debts or arrested for committing crime. The whole thing sickened Joe but he had always struggled to find a way out of the mess of waiting for a giro or nicking from the local shops. He'd been caught a few times but got away with loads too. If you were careful and chose the right times it was a cinch.

Tesco's store car park looked busy at the moment. Looking at the front door from the car park, he could see plenty of people entering and exiting. He squatted down, tucked his Adidas bottoms into his socks and straightened his coat. The trick was to appear natural and not to target the same store too many times in a short space of time. If you became too well known to the staff, the security guard would just track you around the store making it hard for you to nick. They couldn't actually grab you until you were leaving with 'unpaid for goods' but they made it bloody hard to even get that far. Joe hadn't been to this store for nearly six months, so was feeling lucky. He approached the door and dropped his hood back, grabbing a basket from the interior lobby, and entering, noted the security guard straight away; a skinny Asian male whose uniform hung from his frame, looking bored out of his brains as he was approached by an elderly couple with an enquiry. Joe strolled past unnoticed. *Never assume you haven't been seen*, Joe thought to himself.

There were four types of guard that he had encountered in the past, not gender specific. One: 'The Sloth' - skinny and bored but looked incapable of stopping granny shoplifting (he knew a couple of pensioners who loved the challenge!). Two: 'The Blob'- obese, passing the time of day and polite but if I can fill the doors before you, you're not getting out. Three: 'The Wannabe' - professional, I've pressed this uniform, not tried the army or police, but I'm gonna have you if you try it (most dangerous). Finally, four: 'The Ostrich' - incapable of dressing themselves, talking to anyone would be a challenge, stopping a shoplifter, 'you are having a laugh'. Today, Joe had a Sloth but everyone hoped for an Ostrich!

He walked through the fresh fruit area and walked along the back of the store checking to see if he saw anyone he knew or knew him, including off duty coppers. Things looked to be safe, he chucked some pasta and some beans in his basket and headed to the drink aisle.

Things were quiet, no staff. Placing his basket down, as he reached right for G&T and vodka and coke mixed cans, he dropped two down each trouser leg. Picking his basket up, he moved on and scuttled a 75cl of Bell's whisky up his sleeve, moving on to the biscuit aisle as a couple of women walked past him. Checking the tills, he could see they were busy and he cut towards the exit of the store gently placing his basket within the medicines aisle. Looking left, he saw the Sloth exiting the toilets behind the till. He was attempting to fasten his trouser belt, as he struggled to negotiate around his fluorescent vest displaying his role.

*Bloody standards; can't dress in private and probably not even washed his bloody hands. The bloody world's going down the pan*, thought Joe, as he strolled out with 'unpaid for goods' secreted under his clothing.

He walked away from the store and crossed the road heading for a small public garden in the town where he sat down on a bench. Untucking one of his trouser legs, he took out a Vodka coke, which he quickly necked in a pathetic attempt to stop his shakes and cramps. He then continued on to the outskirts of town to one of the pubs which he knew would buy from him. Ten minutes later he walked out of the pub ten pounds the richer, secreted in his right sock, and headed off to score. Only one bag this time, although the Scousers wouldn't need to ask why if they read the papers, no more free bags for him for fetching Fatty Wellbury's drugs for him.

\*\*\*

Rachel and Jones arrived at Barnston Hospital mortuary to speak to the pathologist that had performed the autopsy on Frank Wellbury. Neither had opted to attend the physical event, both believing it unnecessary.

The pathologist was the expert in this field and watching him carefully inspect the body and examine its internal organs, although interesting, didn't interest them enough and neither thought that they could add anything of value to the examination. Best leave the experts to do their thing and report back to them afterwards.

Rachel parked the small blue Vauxhall Corsa and stepped out as Jones peeled himself from the vehicle, the suspension giving a sigh of relief as he climbed out. Both knew the way to the mortuary, walking towards a side hospital door, Rachel buzzed on the intercom, waiting for a reply.

"Bloody hate these places," said Jones.

Rachel made no reply, thinking that she didn't know any people who liked hospitals. They were a place of need for most that were generally having a time of crisis in their lives, cared for by professional and dedicated staff but let's face it, most people wanted to get away from hospitals as quickly as they could.

*Suppose Wellbury's beyond caring*, thought Rachel, as a rather nasal voice responded to the intercom, "Can I help you?"

"D/Supt Jones and DI Barnes from the police, sir," replied Rachel, "You should be expecting us."

"Oh, yes, yes of course. Please come in" replied the intercom, as a long buzz sounded at the door. Rachel pushed open the door and was greeted by warm air, enveloping them with the aroma of cleanliness particular to hospital environments.

"After you, sir," said Rachel, holding the door open for Jones.

"Thank you," he replied, stepping into the building, the age of chivalry abandoned in the importance of this moment. Entering a further internal door, both were welcomed by a tall male wearing grey scrubs and sporting a yellow surgical cap.

"Morning guys, Dr Armitage, pathologist," he introduced himself. Jones reached out to shake hands, stalled by Armitage who raised his hands saying, "Maybe not the best idea," smiling at the officers. "Please come this way." Armitage was tall and slim with dark hair parted to the right and about fifty years old. He had a cultured accent and moved confidently through his domain, as they walked a small corridor entering two-way doors into a cooler environment. Metal cabinets lined one wall, clearly designed to hold cadavers, their polished steel doors all closed, protecting the bodies inside in their cold environment, an empty trolley standing forlornly in front of them. Entering the autopsy room there was a table sat within the centre with a large body thereon, covered in a white sheet. Polished instruments stood on standby on a trolley against a far wall awaiting the precision of Armitage's hands on his next client. Armitage walked to a sink turning on the long handled taps with his elbows, and removing his gloves, commenced scrubbing his hands.

"Can never be too careful," he said, smiling at them both.

"Right, initial autopsy complete," he started as he dried his hands on a paper towel walking towards the body, "I'll save you all the preamble as you'll get that in my report and just get down to the nitty gritty. Examination of the body so far indicates to me that the cause of death is primarily chemical asphyxiation, likely preceded by a Class A overdose of morphine or heroin," he clarified. "These would both be consistent with the circumstances in which you found the body," he continued as he walked towards the body, pulling back the white sheet at the left arm.

"Look here," he indicated a small mark on the inside

of the elbow. "A small pinprick in the left antecubital fossa with apparent underlying trauma to the vein, indicating an injection site. No other injection sites found on the body." Covering the arm back up, he then moved to the head, pulling back the sheet and revealing Wellbury's face. "You are aware of the material within the mouth, which I have now removed. On examination, I can tell you they are a pair of red socks which were balled up and forced into the oral cavity and partially beyond the epiglottis." Armitage reached for a kidney dish which contained the saliva stained socks. "I assume you will want these as an exhibit," he said, as he placed them back down, smiling. "Looking at his face you can see the cyanosis, blue tinge, and the petechia. The petechiae are also present on the surface of his eyes, scalp and heart." Armitage opened Wellbury's eye, which was bloodshot and pointed to small red veins on the eye, face and scalp, looking like a spider's intricate trail of burst capillaries. He spared showing them the heart. "The sides of the mouth by the lips are torn. There are no defensive marks on the body indicating a fight. There are other internal indications, which will be detailed in my report, which generally indicate starvation of oxygen. Toxicology will be forthcoming and will clarify my findings," he finished.

Rachel looked at Jones, who nodded. "So, Dr Armitage, what is your hypothesis?"

"Oh, undoubtedly you have a murder," he replied, with a tinge of excitement. "Your victim has taken or been given a high dose of heroin intravenously. No syringe has been found at the scene. When slouched and comatose, the socks have been stuffed down his throat by an unknown party, causing asphyxiation," he concluded, covering up Wellbury's face. "I'll get my report finished and emailed to your office. All clothes and personal effects have been exhibited by my assistant Martin, indicating to a man standing at the other side of the door. If I can be of any further assistance, please contact me but now I have to run to a meeting upstairs." Armitage directed them to Martin, who came in to show both the officers outside.

Outside of the hospital, they returned to the car and Rachel turned the engine on, Jones remaining quiet and contemplative.

"What do you think, Boss?" asked Rachel.

"Confirmation of some things that we thought, Rachel. We need to strengthen some lines of enquiry too, though. Who is his heroin supplier? On the face of it we have a guy who abuses heroin by smoking it but now we have an injection site. Socks rammed in his mouth but he was wearing a pair and no clothes lying around so where did they come from? We need the CCTV from his house – what's that going to tell us? Loads to do Rachel, loads to do. Let's get back to the nick and see where we are with the enquiries."

Rachel manoeuvred the vehicle out of the hospital grounds and headed back towards Barnston nick.

***

It was three o'clock and Joe still hadn't managed to score. The Tommy line hadn't been switched on yet and all the smackheads in town were waiting for their fixes. Joe had passed small gatherings of them in town, their pale faces and emaciated bodies huddled as they clubbed money together to get the maximum amount of bags. They'd all stab each other in the back, in a blink, but when they needed to score, all became best mates. 'Tommy' when he or she appeared could be anybody. All the Scousers called themselves 'Tommy'. Happy in the success of their business model they could make everyone wait as long as they liked. You either waited or didn't get served, it made little difference to them, as they knew you'd always come back. When the drug syndicate were ready, a group text would be sent out from a 'hub' phone in Merseyside, held by a middleman letting the users know they were out and dealing. Word of mouth would find their location as the users scurried like trained rats towards their fix. Joe would wait for the text but during the past few months hadn't needed to club with the others, as Wellbury had funded his habit whilst he had scored on his behalf. 'Tommy' knew of Wellbury, though wouldn't give a toss about his present demise. There would always be another Wellbury in the town for them to profit from. Joe received his text and headed down to the beach from the south side cliff where he had been waiting. The wind still blew brusquely cutting through his coat, chilling the cold sweat on his skin. The dealers frequently changed their locations, always choosing a place where they believed that they could see the cops coming and get away from them, should they do so. Joe was on alert but the likelihood of cops being around would be small. Every now and again the police would arrest a dealer but in all honesty it was ineffective. Yes, they would get an arrest, in all likelihood a juvenile; if they were lucky, they would find some drugs but with a no comment interview would then spend more time putting a file together to satisfy the Crime Prosecution Service than it took to conduct the arrest. At best, the dealing would stop for two to three hours whilst the syndicate sent another 'Tommy' by train to the coast to restart the dealing and the circle would start again. He continued towards the beach, watching a couple of users trailing back. He didn't want this life of living hand to mouth, scraping money together for the next bag and shooting it into his veins. Wellbury was maybe better off dead, even his wealth didn't hold back the ravages of the modern world. Joe got out his tenner, wishing for the oblivion that the evening would bring once he'd completed one more job.

***

Mount Way at six o'clock, Sebastian Briggs of Briggs and Watson Law Firm strolled along the South Cliff towards the direction of his home address, following his regular dalliance at Brooks Bar. Under his beige raincoat, he wore a trim pinstripe three piece suit with black patent leather shoes, clicking along, and a black rolled up umbrella, used as a walking stick. He was the perfect gent, his brown shoulder length hair swept back by the now oncoming breeze. Another day spent earning a fortune in legal aid from the world's unfortunates who found themselves in police custody. Petty criminals loved him – 'always beat the pigs with slippery Briggs' was a well-known phrase throughout their friends. If you got nicked, he was the first name to ask for. Many were on first name terms with him and the police disliked him. He always seemed to get people off; rumours had it that he was a crook himself who regularly was paid with cocaine. No smoke without fire, but nothing proven.

Watching again from the shadows of a tree, a figure observed Briggs, once again on his usual route home, walking Mount Way, his timing like clockwork. Thursday was always an office day for Briggs and he took the same route home every day with an adulterous halt at one of the South Cliff bars on his way home to his wife and kids. Men like him making a living from the vulnerable and needy and living life according to his own rules. It was sickening. The figure turned and walked back towards the town. *I will have to see what can be done about him*, the figure thought to themselves.

# Chapter 3

## February 1985

Richard Greaves woke up in the bedroom he shared with his two brothers in their three bedroom semi, on a council estate in Barnston. The room was the only one on the second floor, a converted loft space with no central heating, just a lonely oil-filled electric heater at one end of the room, struggling against the inescapable fact that it was losing the battle. The single glazed windows were frosted on the inside with a thin layer of ice, which slowly crept upwards from the windowsill towards the woodchip papered ceiling, their crystalline patterns fracturing the daylight. Painted white, the ceiling sloped from its apex in both directions where it encountered the white painted woodchip walls. The room was not elaborate, with Richard's parents short on cash and imagination, but it was kept clean and functional. One end of the room was 'owned' by Richard's eldest brother and was not currently occupied, with the divan single bed undisturbed. Posters of ELO, Genesis, and Gabriel adorned the walls and, suspiciously, Kate Bush looking down from the ceiling!

Richard shared his end of the room with his brother. A wooden staircase entered at their end of the room with a wooden rail preventing a dangerous fall. On the wall at the top of the stairs, a hand painted map of Tolkien's Middle Earth, the lonely mountain taking precedence on the woodchip. Richard checked his Timex, the hands indicating 7 am, took a deep breath and got quickly into his trackies, T-shirt and hand knitted jumper. His other brother, older again, lay wrapped under his duvet in the security of the warmth, eyes closed. Richard quietly went down the stairs through his parent's bedroom, the bed empty, the room cramped and crammed with wardrobe, clothes and generalised hoarded household wares. Entering the living room, the coal fire was already lit, his father tending to it before he set off to work, his mother sat in a chair, coffee and fag in hand.

"Morning," Richard said quietly, to be greeted by a smile from his mother, in her voluminous cloud of smoke, and a hand wave from his father. Richard's father was picking up a home-made packet of coal 'dust' wrapped in newspaper and placing it on the fire. Every evening his father would go out to the coal shed, within the garage, and collect the dust (dross, he would call it) from the bunker and with wet newspaper make a package to place on the fire, claiming that it would burn for ages and save money. Money was tight but the monotonous predictability of his actions would send his mother spare and frequently assisted in being the catalyst for a parental argument. Richard walked through the living room, "Off to do the papers," he said, walking through the small kitchen into the garage and out into the world to complete his paper round.

Richard walked out on to the top road where red brick houses lined either side, thrown together and hunched protectively against the estate's thugs, some occupied and others boarded up with council metal grilles to prevent damage and theft. Insufficient to prevent the needy from ripping them open and removing kitchen units, sinks and boilers or copper piping which would fetch a good price at the 'scrappies'. Richard headed right towards a small turning circle and an alley, which would give him a quick route through the estate, to the shop where he would order and fetch his papers. He loved this time of day, with the streets still relatively quiet, the sun bathing roofs gently in a warm embrace and no one to challenge, confront or frighten him. Walking through the alleyways he crossed the second and first rows of the estate and emerged near the community centre, where a smashed up red Ford Escort sat despondently, number plate missing, tyres flat and exhaust ripped off. Richard walked to the rear garage of the shop and opened the door, stepping in to put his papers in order.

"Morning John," said Richard to the shop owner and received, "Richard" in reply.

Picking a clipboard up, Richard checked and ordered the newspapers before putting them into a yellow fluorescent bag. Only thirty papers to deliver, but the longest route, for which he got paid five pounds a week. He grabbed the shop bike and headed off to the South Cliff of Barnston. This was his time, freedom, no hassles and still a couple of hours until he would have to face school.

One hour later, Richard had finished his round, dropped the bike and bag at the shop and now walked into the family home where his father had gone to work, the fire smoked slowly (dross package in place) and his mother remained somewhere within her miasma of nicotine, her slippered toes poking from under the cloud. Richard nipped upstairs and changed into a school uniform; a blazer decorated with the school emblem on the breast pocket and looked the smartest that he ever did. These were the smartest clothes he had, even though they were hand-me-downs. He was one of the 'blazer boys' – the kids who always went to school in the correct uniform, never daring enough to deviate, always trying to stay in line, no detentions, break no rules, anonymous. Richard didn't dislike school itself but it challenged him mentally and socially. He didn't fit in and kids could be vicious in the right circumstances. He grabbed a slice of toast and a glass of milk and went to the bathroom. Looking back from the mirror was a red, irritated, acne covered face which he hated, with pale blue eyes and slightly greasy hair which was parted to the right. He washed with cold water, no soap, and none of the medicinal face soaps that other kids could afford. Drying his face, he straightened his tie, thin end on display and kipper end tucked behind his buttoned white shirt, and said to his image, "Right, here we go. Stand up to Wellbury, don't let him beat you." He smiled unconvincingly and headed out the door to school.

Richard headed towards the turning circle alleyway where, sat on a low garden wall, a couple of lads from the estate were sitting smoking a hand rolled cigarette, the sweet smell of cannabis loitering in the air around them. Both lads were in their teens, one dark haired, the other with dirty blond hair. Looking back up the road, Richard spotted Rogers, the local beat bobby, walking in their general direction.

"Cops," he warned them. The cig was docked, pocketed and both stood up, seeing Rogers as he spotted them.

"Here we go," dark hair laughed, giving Rogers a wave as they moved towards the alleyway. Rogers threw his police helmet and started off at speed towards them. Dark hair entered the alleyway.

"See you later," he nodded towards his mate, picking up his pace.

"Wanted for skipping his bail," said blond hair to Richard. "Rogers will never catch him," he continued, as the police officer sprinted past shouting, "Look after my hat I'll be back for it."

"Will do, plod," blond hair replied, smiling.

Walking back up the road, blond hair retrieved the police helmet, which had come to a rest against a garden brick wall, its pristine brushed black material now marked with mud. Blond placed it on his head and marching up to Richard said in a superior voice, "You are under arrest."

Richard looked agog as the lad laughed, taking off the helmet.

"Only joking, mate. Rogers isn't that bad but he'll be back for this," as he held the helmet out. Looking at the helmet, Richard could see that it was cared for, with a silver coloured crest on the front and Yorkshire rose on the top, polished and gleaming.

"Looks a bit too neat though don't it," stated blond, "We can soon alter that," he continued, passing the helmet to Richard to hold. Richard, feeling intimidated, took the helmet.

"Right mate, quickly now, smash the top of it in. Rogers won't know he didn't do it himself when he threw it, but we will," he said, winking at Richard.

"I don't know," Richard replied, "what if he comes back?"

"Just do it," the blonde replied, moving closer in, gently clenching his fists.

"Now," he said quietly, leaning his face in towards Richard's.

Richard stepped back, raising the helmet. This was bloody stupid but he was scared, scared in the same way that Wellbury scared him at school. Backing away but raising the helmet, in anger and frustration he smashed it down flattening the rose on the top. He chucked the helmet at blondie and ran to the sounds of him laughing in his wake, holding his own tears of disappointment to himself. He didn't care about damaging the helmet; it was letting himself be forced into it that hurt. It was in being so scared, that he just folded and did what he was told to do. It was not fighting back. He felt pathetic.

Exiting the alley, now walking, he saw PC Rogers slowly walking up the hill beyond the alleyway to the top road, hands empty and dark hair nowhere to be seen. Richard turned left, ensuring he avoided Rogers and continued his route to school, leaving the estate. What a bloody start, he thought to himself but stuff it, one against the establishment, even if it was only damaging some policeman's hat, he thought feebly.

***

Barnston Methodist School stood ominously, its multifaceted windows looking down at Richard as he approached. School buses stood, engines rumbling, in a long line as they waited their turn to enter the school grounds and deposit their occupants. Faces on board laughing and smiling, sulking or lost in a world of music listened to on Sony Walkmans. Kids walked into school in clusters, weighty school bags crammed with books and PE kits, ready to take on the challenges of the day. A cold day with a relentless wind stealing round corners, flicking scrunchied high ponytails, crimped to perfection, coiffured centre partings and the occasional stiffly gelled flat top. The whiff of cheap perfume and aftershave occasionally scented the air within the school grounds and teachers shuffled towards their staff rooms, heads down, avoiding pupil engagement until the onslaught of the day's activities.

Richard entered the school gates in trepidation, eyes scanning for danger, in full fight or flight mode. If he could just get through to his form without seeing Wellbury, he would be safe for a while. He could sneak down to the sports hall and hide down there until the nine o'clock bell, which was only five minutes away. The only kids down there would be sneaking in a quick cigarette before lessons or boyfriends and girlfriends who, struggling with an evening's abstinence, were now snogging the faces off each other. School for Richard was enforced anguish. The lesson times themselves were reasonable and although he struggled with many lessons, they were preferable to the torture of break times, which he would spend in solitude, sneaking around the school and hiding in corners. Not every day was like this but there were too many days that he spent in fear. The school bell sounded and Richard made it to form safely; his day at school had begun.

Mr McDermott sat waiting at his desk for his form to file in and take their seats at their desks. He was the school's German teacher, skinny of form, with a predominant Adam's apple, which floated up and down his throat, his guttural enunciations in the 'Mother Tongue' enforced upon the kids as they entered the classroom. Richard's morning went fine with history, his vertically challenged, bearded teacher, resembling Thorin Oakenshield, reading rote from a hefty tome. Next, geography; Mr Gott had an uncanny ability to draw any map on the blackboard freehand with no reference guide. Mr Gott also had piercing pale blue eyes which bored into you when asking a question, as if daring you to hold his stare. Nobody could. The bell went off at lunch time. Richard packed away his books and prepared himself for the coliseum of the school grounds.

*\*\**

The school dining room was packed, a queue to the door, with boisterous pupils pushing in and pushing past in an attempt to try to get some sort of decent food before the chips ran out. The kids with a pack up sat clustered around three tables, wishing for the freedom of the school dinner instead of beef paste sandwiches, an apple, and a milk jelly, provided by parents trying hard to balance budgets. Richard walked past the windows by himself, warily avoiding an environment where he may have to socialise or fight his way to an empty seat, which he would swiftly get evicted from by someone popular. He walked around the corner of the building and... *Oh no*, Frank Wellbury and his posse were walking towards him.

Wellbury spotted him straight away and at five foot ten, broad shouldered and weighty, laughed and walked straight at Richard.

"Hey there, Dick, you loser, how are you doing?" said Wellbury, placing his arm across Richard's shoulders, squeezing him in a friendly hug and giving him a painful noogie. Richard tried to squirm away.

"Get off, you git," said Richard, struggling more as Wellbury grabbed his backpack. Wellbury's friends just stood back, laughing at the little kid attempting to shove Wellbury back.

"Whoa! A little fight in you today is there, Dick?" laughed Wellbury, clipping Richard over the back of his head with a right hand slap.

"Get off!" shouted Richard in anger and frustration. Wellbury laughed, preparing to dole out another smack, when suddenly he was shouldered off balance and into a wall.

"Sorry, mate, didn't see you there," said Matthew Forster, who had, apparently innocently, walked around the corner of the building and bumped into Wellbury. Matthew was tall and lithe and stood with his arms open apologetically, his little sidekick Joe Marsden standing next to him.

"Really sorry, I was in a rush to get to the sports hall, Frank; we've got double rugby next." Joe turned to Richard, who now stood to one side,

"Bugger off," he said, gesturing to the main school

building. Richard wasted no time, his face reddening in embarrassment.

"Watch where you're going Forster?" replied Wellbury, having regained his balance.

Matthew just looked straight at Wellbury, winked and walked past, Joe following behind, in the general direction of the sports changing rooms. Wellbury stood nonplussed and with no Richard to pick on, gathered his cronies and followed towards the sports hall.

Fifteen minutes later all the lads left the changing rooms pushing and shoving and ran towards the rugby pitch, wearing black shorts, black and red striped rugby shirts with their studs clicking on the concrete path like crazed tap dancers. Wellbury was running with the forwards, Matthew and Joe with the backs. Bringing up the rear was the disconsolate skinny figure of Richard in a top that swamped him and socks pulled over his knees. He was freezing, hated the game and wasn't looking forward to getting a battering. The sports teacher Mr Sanderson bounced out of the changing rooms.

"Come on lads, with me," he shouted, as he started running the circumference of the field with an obligatory 'warm up', then straight into running and passing drills followed by scrimmaging. Thirty minutes later, it was time for a match. Sanderson had split the sides evenly and stood in the middle waiting to toss a coin for the start.

"Wellbury, Greaves up you come," shouted Sanderson, totally oblivious of their personal, or lack of personal, relationship. Wellbury walked up, knees and face covered in mud, having got stuck in on the drills. Richard walked up wearing an orange bib (designated to his side) which hung down to his pristine white knees, looking dwarfed by Wellbury. The coin was tossed with Wellbury's side winning.

"See you soon, Dick," Wellbury said, smiling at Richard who turned, shoulders hunched and walked disconsolately back to his teammates.

"Right, on my whistle," shouted Sanderson excitedly, as he paced towards Richard's receiving team, arm held out to the side. Richard turned to the opposition to see Wellbury speaking to his fly-half, who held the ball ready to kick. The whistle blew. The ball was kicked. Richard looked up, tracking its trajectory.

"No, no, no" he mumbled, as the ball flew down towards him, an Exocet missile on its flight path. Arms held out from his chest, held together in their collection cup and the quickening sound of thunder as booted feet headed his way. The ball dropped lower.

"Catch it, catch it!" screamed his team. The moment slowed, the ball dropped, Richard grimaced, the ball hit his arms and he pulled it into his chest.

"Got it!" he yelled, as Wellbury's shoulder collided with his mid torso, smashing him to the turf, his face mashing into the mud as bodies piled on top. Richard held on and twisted, trying to place the ball back but Wellbury held him, digging a fist into his ribs. The whistle blew as Wellbury's forearm trapped Richard's neck unseen by Sanderson in the melee. The whistle blew louder and play stopped. Bodies peeled off each other, revealing Richard flattened, Wellbury's hand using Richard's face innocently as a prop, as he slowly stood up.

"Failure to release on the tackle, Frank. Tackle and roll away. Penalty to bibs," said Sanderson, raising his arm to affirm his decision.

Richard rolled the ball away and slowly standing, was helped by Matthew.

"Well held, Greaves, you took that tackle well," said Matthew, collecting the ball ready for the penalty.

Richard smiled and for the first time for a long time at school, felt proud of himself. Complimented by the school team captain and he'd done something right. *Maybe this game wasn't so bad.*

Richard's opinion soon changed, as time after time Wellbury smashed into him, clearly targeting him and hurting him, Richard holding back his tears.

"I'm sick of this," Matthew said quietly to Joe. "Next time you get the ball, lose it to Fatty, I'll be with you."

A line out was won by the bibs as the ball spun out. Joe received and ran towards Wellbury. Slipping he flipped the ball up into Wellbury's path, a look of glee on Fatty's face, as he intercepted and charged forward. A lithe figure launched towards him in a high tackle as a bibbed shoulder connected with his chin then... nothing! The whistle blew.

Matthew peeled himself off Wellbury, who lay temporarily unconscious on the grass, arms flung wide with weighty midriff exposed.

"Sorry, sorry," said Matthew loudly, "misjudged tackle, he's OK, isn't he?" in a panicked voice. Sanderson ran in as Wellbury stirred, sitting up.

"Stay sat, son. Accidental high tackle, Matthew you should know better. We'll get you to the office and call the nurse, Frank. The rest of you, get to the changing rooms, showered and off when the bell sounds."

The muddied lads turned, jogging back to the changing rooms, all chatting, some smirking, Matthew winking at Joe as he went past him.

Richard suffered the obligatory embarrassment of shared showers and left the sports block with everyone else in their cloud of Denim and Kouros. The school day had ended and Richard had survived. Forster had helped him today and he wouldn't forget that. Richard hadn't defended himself as he had wished, but he had told

Wellbury to "Get off" and he'd tried on the rugby pitch. Small victories. Fatty had got what he deserved though, thought Richard, smiling as he headed on his way home.

# Chapter 4

Rachel arrived home at seven o'clock, to be greeted by Matthew, who had a bottle of Merlot breathing, two Bordeaux glasses stood in anticipation. Outside, it was getting colder and the embrace provided by the warm air of the log burner was comforting as well as the warm cuddle and kiss provided by Matthew. The range cooker was humming; a sensual aroma of garlic infused the kitchen originating from a Le Creuset casserole dish which bubbled on the cooker hob, a pan of potatoes burbling cheerfully next to it.

"How's it been?" asked Matthew sympathetically, "You must be bloody knackered."

"Hard work and yes I am. Thanks for all this," she said, gesturing to the wine and cooker, smiling at him.

"Anything for Detective Inspector Barnes," he replied, "There's a hot bath ready upstairs for you. Dinner will be ready when you are done. Go and jump in then you can tell me all about your day." Matthew handed her a poured glass of wine, taken gratefully, and Rachel headed upstairs. She stripped off and walked into a steamy bathroom, lowering into the hot water as it enveloped her body.

"What a day!" she said to herself as she ran it all through in her head. She was physically tired but her mind was buzzing with investigation. All the work to do, the lines of enquiry, poor Frank Wellbury dead and somewhere out there, a killer. A murderer, that she had to catch and build a case to ensure that he or she was brought to justice. This is why she joined the police. You didn't get a bigger job than a murder. Rachel dunked her head back, soaking her hair and after soaking her body, dried herself and chucked on some comfortable pyjamas. Now feeling refreshed, she went downstairs to enjoy a meal and some time with Matt.

Rachel walked into the kitchen, where Matt had laid out plates and cutlery for their meal, serving up chicken in a red wine sauce, potatoes, carrots and peas. Basic cookery that smelt and looked wonderful.

"Thanks," said Rachel, smiling. "How's your day been?"

"Forget my day," replied Matthew excitedly, "how's yours been? Murder eh! In the thick of it; finding clues; chasing down the suspect; looking for an arrest, it's just like telly." he finished in a broad Yorkshire accent. "Come on, spill the beans."

"You know I can't, Matt. It's all confidential."

"Of course you can. It's me! I'm not going to say anything. I might even be able to help. Holmes and Watson or even Barnes and Forster," he gestured as if their names were in lights. "It's Wellbury eh, murdered. I heard it was heroin," he continued.

Rachel frowned. "How'd you hear that?" she asked him.

"Aha! There you go you see, you're not the only one who knows things. Can't divulge my sources," he replied conspiratorially. Rachel looked at Matt closely.

"What else do you know, then?" she asked him.

"There you go, you've confirmed it," he smiled, slapping his hands together. "Told you I could help. So it was heroin. What's he done? Overdosed? Who would have thought that a fat git like him used heroin? They're usually skinny little rats scratching around the streets, not local businessmen. I wonder how he got onto it?" Matthew continued, getting into his rhythm.

"I haven't confirmed anything," Rachel smiled, rolling her eyes.

"Yes, you have and you know it," he replied. "What else then? An overdose isn't usually a murder, just a tragic accident. What makes this a murder?"

"You are incorrigible," Rachel laughed, squinting her eyes at him and poking him across the table.

"Come on," he replied, "you know you want to."

Rachel frowned, thinking that this was going to be a busy few months in which she'd need Matt's support. Her job would demand more and more from her and Matt would have to put up with more long days and an absence of her in body and spirit, the unheralded support that many police officers needed: the support of a strong partner at home. *Stuff it, he's safe and will keep it to himself*, she thought.

"OK, OK. I give in but you've got to keep it to yourself or I'll lose my job," said Rachel seriously.

"Yes, Ma'am, OK" Matthew replied, calming and looking straight at her.

"Yes, it is Wellbury; the press will confirm that tomorrow anyway. What they don't know is that it is heroin and that ..." she contemplated "... he was choked with a pair of socks shoved in his throat," she finished. There it was, she'd told him.

Matt sat back, mouth slightly open with a confused look on his face, trying to picture the image.

"That's just bloody weird," he said to Rachel.

"You're telling me," she replied.

They continued talking, with Rachel refusing to disclose anything else about the case, despite Matt's attempts to squirrel more from her. She tactfully steered the conversation away from police work, talking about the weekend to come and things to do in the house.

Later, Rachel turned over in bed, back to Matthew, absolutely tired out and slightly worse for wear with the wine. It was a trip to headquarters in the morning. Closing her eyes, she wondered how Matt had known about the heroin overdose and knowing that she'd told him too much, hoped she wouldn't regret it.

***

The following morning, Rachel drove Jones back from headquarters after a meeting that he had had with his Chief Superintendent. Jones was speaking on the phone to one of his colleagues.

"Bloody woman," he said, "sticking her nose in, trying to tell me what to do. Honestly, she hasn't got a bloody clue, Geoff, no clue at all. How she got to Chief Super I have no idea - she is bloody useless. Probably shagged her way there," he laughed in response to something Geoff had said, looking at Rachel and realising he was in female company.

"Anyway, got to go, I'm just getting to the nick. Speak soon." With that, he terminated the call and placed the phone in his pocket.

"That's us here," he smiled at Rachel. She concentrated as she swiftly parallel parked the car into an empty space behind the nick.

"Amazing!" mumbled Jones to himself.

"What was that, sir?" asked Rachel. "Was that amazing you said?" Jones stepped out of the car, closing the door.

"Well, you wouldn't normally get that from a woman," he replied "You know, parallel parking in one move, indeed, being able to park correctly at all. Quite extraordinary," he smiled as he closed the door. Rachel looked at his turned back and mouthed "arse," closing her door. She approached the rear door of the police station, opening it for Jones, who stepped forward. Rachel allowed it to close slightly and looking at Jones said, "Oh sorry sir, you probably wouldn't expect a woman to open a door for you would you, that prerogative obviously being a man's." She smiled at him, stepped in front of Jones and entered, the door starting to close behind her, forcing Jones to grab it quickly before it closed fully. Rachel continued towards an interior door and entered, which again was closing behind her, forcing Jones to run and catch it to enter himself. Both climbed the stairs towards the Major Incident Room (MIR) and upon entering the corridor Jones stated, "Rachel, in my office first, please." He walked in, followed by Rachel, closing the door behind her.

"Look Rachel, I'm sorry," Jones started, "I'm under a lot of pressure on this one and if I've talked out of turn, I apologise."

"If you've talked out of turn!" Rachel replied incredulously, glaring at him. "Respectfully sir, we are both under a lot of pressure but that doesn't justify YOU acting like a chauvinistic idiot. This organisation is full of chauvinistic dinosaurs paying lip service to equality; please don't be one of them. I'm here because I am good and you know that. I'm not here to be talked to like that," she finished.

"OK, OK I deserve that," replied Jones, holding arms out placatingly. "I'll do my best not to be a T-Rex and please accept my apology. You are good and I was out of order. It won't happen again."

Rachel stood, face calm, inside surprised at his comments and her own frankness in speaking her thoughts. He had disarmed her though, with an honest apology.

"OK" she replied, as there was a firm knock on the door.

Andy's head popped round the door

"You'll want to come with me, guys," he said, smiling. "Possible break through with CCTV." Andy held the door open, Rachel took hold of it and all headed into the Major Incident Room.

***

The MIR was located on the same floor of the building behind a secure door. On entering the room, there were various people working at different computer terminals set in three rows within the office. The computers held the software for the Holmes system on which the Force recorded all their murder enquiries allowing them to track all actions and link enquiries. Holmes was run by a team who were experts in the system and would be vital to the investigation and was named after Sir Arthur Conan Doyle's legendary detective, Sherlock. At the rear of the room, two officers sat at computers which were used to research all CCTV brought into the investigation. The first task the officers would have been given was to identify all CCTV within a given parameter, in this case being Wellbury's private CCTV, all public CCTV within Palmerston View, all private CCTV at residential or commercial premises within the street and all the same for any natural foot or vehicular route into the street. The officers would then create actions which were given to enquiry teams; to go out and collect the CCTV in a format capable of being reviewed within the MIR and then supply it in this format to the reviewing officers. The same process was used for all enquiries to ensure a logical and controlled progression throughout the investigation. Researching and reviewing CCTV was an onerous task but could often yield lines of enquiries to the investigation which were invaluable. The officers started with reviewing the CCTV from 119 Palmerston, that being the easiest and quickest to collect and clear logic indicated that Wellbury had been killed at home and therefore his murderer must have attended the house in order to commit the offence.

Andy walked towards the back of the room, followed by Jones and Rachel. Officers at their desks looked up but continued their work, they were busy and would get used to the management wandering through when they needed to. They all walked towards the CCTV reviewing officers.

"OK guys, show the bosses what you have found," said Andy to them both.

"OK sir," replied one, taking the lead, and started with an explanation.

"So, we have started reviewing the CCTV from Palmerston. It's a reasonable digital system which we've downloaded. The system works in colour and has a night-time capability, where it switches to black and white. The victim has CCTV at the front and rear doors, also one covering the garage door and his car at the top of the drive and another facing down the driveway to the front gates. All cameras run on a twenty four hour loop system recorded digitally, which self-erases and commences recording again at 7 pm every evening." Jones and Rachel waited patiently, allowing the officer to build to his moment of glory in his revelation of what had been found. Inside Rachel wanted to say, "Just bloody show me!" but she respected the hard work that had been put in here, so held her tongue.

The officer carried on, "We used two twenty on the morning of the death as a starting point, as that is when CSI can be seen attending the scene." The officer then turned on the screen and showed on the screen a clear black and white image, split into five screens of all of the CCTV covering number 119. It was ten o'clock at night, which showed digitally at the top left of the screen, the date underneath.

"Check the gate image first, then the car, then the front door. I'll play it at a slower speed but watch closely." The officer played the footage.

At 10.01 a person wearing a dark coat, fur lined hood up, approached the gate and an arm reached up to buzz the intercom. The image was 'fuzzy' and at a distance and from the movement of the laurels, the wind was picking up and there was rain sweeping from right to left. The gates opened and the person walked past the gate and up the drive.

"A man," stated Jones. The person walked beyond the car.

"Stop there, rewind five seconds," said Rachel. The officer complied.

"Stop. Look there," she pointed, "White writing on the right sleeve and at the back of the neck."

"Yes," said Jones, leaning in.

The footage continued, with all eyes on the front door. The figure appeared towards the door, head looking down and slowly raising as the figure approached. The air was tense around the computer, breath held and white knuckled hands gripping chair backs. On screen, the area lit up as an exterior light was activated and light from an open doorway spilled onto the screen. The figure stepped up, where it was frozen in place by the officer, showing the gaunt white chin and nose of a white male, clean shaven, the glint of something below eye level, upper face obstructed by the hood, and clearly on the front left breast of the coat the word 'Rockport'.

"We have ourselves a suspect," said Jones beaming. "Nice one, lads, nice one."

\*\*\*

Richard had got up early this morning, ate his customary bowl of porridge and drank a cup of Yorkshire tea, before heading out of the dingy little ground floor flat that he lived in on the south side of Barnston. The flat resembled a 'granny' flat with a door opening into a small dull little living room; leading off from there, a bedroom and bathroom and from the bedroom, a door to a small kitchen. The layout of the flat was unusual but rent was cheap and Richard didn't need much space. A second-hand sofa and chair, a small dining table and chair filled the living room in company with a twenty-eight inch television sat upon a set of cheap bedside drawers. The carpet was light brown and one enlarged photograph, showing the sea crashing into the lighthouse at Barnston harbour, adorned one wall. The room was sparse but clean. The bedroom contained a single bed, wardrobe and bookcase, again all clean, the bed made and bookcase ordered. Richard loved reading, his choice of books eclectic. A notebook and pen sat together on top of the case with a small pile of books by authors Dan Brown, Jodi Picoult and Ian Rankin. The shelves contained a mixture of classics, local history, medical reference and a wide selection of fiction. The kitchen was clean and small with crockery and utensils for one and the bathroom held a solitary toothbrush. Richard was a single man.

Locking the door and checking his digital watch illuminating the dial, he would have to hurry up in order to catch his train to Fenchurch; zipping up a dark blue Regatta waterproof and adjusting his backpack, he set off down the hill at a small jog. The streets were quiet, dawn just beginning to break; if he jogged and walked at a brisk pace he'd be there in time. Now climbing the hill up towards the rear of the station Richard saw a marked police car driving towards him, probably heading towards their local morning cafe stop for the early shift breakfast snack. As they approached, Richard slowed to a walk with hands in pocket. The vehicle slowed on approach, he could see the officers looking at him, feeling paranoid at their stares, and gave them a feeble smile. The front seat passenger raised her hand in greeting and the vehicle moved off with Richard continuing on his walk.

Bloody police, he thought to himself. Richard had had a couple of run-ins with the police in his past so always felt a paranoia on seeing them. He thought most people probably did. Whenever he had been in a car in the past, with a friend or colleague, they immediately slowed down when a police car was behind them, even if they weren't doing anything wrong. In-built paranoia that seemed instilled in innocent people as well as the guilty. Society was a mess.

Richard reached the station and walked into the immediate chilled air that is present in all railway platforms. He already had his monthly pass so walked straight on to the train from the platform and claimed a double seat tucked at the end of the carriage. He placed his backpack on the single seat next to him to discourage anyone sitting next to him. He loved this journey through the countryside to the city, the gentle roll of the train and the rhythmic sound of the wheels on the track, as he travelled along in the warm compartment. Leaning his head on the window, he watched the guard raise a flag and whistle. The train pulled forward slowly out of the mouth of the station, gaining speed as it headed to the outskirts of the town, where it would stop briefly at a small minor station, collect some passengers and then continue its route to Fenchurch. Richard knew the small station well and had frequently alighted there to visit his one-time and only girlfriend. He shook himself from his reverie of times best forgotten.

The train travelled through the Vale of Yorkshire, an

area of outstanding natural beauty, the countryside worthy of its title. Riverbanks began to emerge from a smothering mist that choked the light. On fading it would reveal the beauty of the river and the small green swathes of shoots trying to mature under the empty branches of woodland. A heron, disturbed by the train, lifted into the air, having been perched upon a tree limb, half sunk in the river, its elegant neck pushed forward as its wings flapped forcing it forward, gliding above the water and disappearing into the far misted bank. This journey always settled Richard's body and mind. Twenty minutes later, Richard could see Fenchurch Cathedral towering over the city, its watchful eye guarding the souls of the city. Checking his bag, Richard ensured that he had his name tag, wallet and gloves and prepared himself to leave the train, which would get to the station in about ten minutes, confirmed by the conductor in his nasal voice.

"This train will shortly be arriving in Fenchurch. Can all passengers ensure that they have all their property when leaving the train; next station Fenchurch."

Richard gave it five minutes and then got up and stood at the carriage intersection, waiting for the train to pull in. The single track ran over a bridge spanning the river and multiple other tracks appeared on the approach to the station. The train slowed gently, brakes squeaking, and came to a halt at platform one. Richard waited for the doors to unlock and stepped out onto the chilly platform. Now daylight, the station was getting busier, with commuters striding their way down platforms, across the bridge, into and out of the station on their mandatory routes to work. Normal and predictable and to Richard, all of it quite boring. Another monotonous day in Richard's life, his enjoyment of the train ride to work complete, now along with the other commuters, he walked down the platform towards the river, where he would use a bridge to cross and trudge his route to work. A little man in a big world; a world which he would love to change.

Richard departed the platform and turned left towards the river, walking over the bridge that would lead him to the hospital. The river was high and the houses down either side had their flood gates closed. A couple of suited cyclists rode the cycle path to town, helmeted heads tucked into shoulders against the oncoming wind, thumbs ready on bike bells to warn pedestrians of their approach. Running down the opposite bank, a Lycra-clad lady jogged slowly towards the bridge, her exhalations of breath visible in the cold morning air. A muffled call of "pull" sounded out and looking down, Richard observed a coxed four glide under the bridge, its four-person team in training. Having crossed the bridge, Richard took the streets to the hospital grounds. Entering the grounds, the footpath passed beside the psychiatric hospital, from where he could head to the side entrance of the general hospital and a staff changing room.

Entering the curtilage of the hospital, Richard placed his lanyard with name tag on and headed into the building. Even at this time, a dressing gowned patient supporting a drip inhaled gratefully on a cigarette foiling the efforts and care given by NHS staff. He walked past the woman saying nothing and entered the hospital with a familiar clinical scent infusing the atmosphere. Richard, head down, then entered the staff changing room, having used the door pass code. Rows of grey metal lockers confronted him and to the right, neatly folded scrubs in grey, green and blue lay on open shelves, underneath which were empty white gurneys waiting to receive used but medically 'clean' scrubs. He grabbed a blue set and headed towards his locker. Various lockers were open, with outdoor coats and bags hanging off them, some with doctors' white coats, stethoscopes dangling from pockets, hanging too. This was a safe environment, secure from the general public and from any potential thieves. The room was empty at the moment, which allowed Richard to change into the blue scrubs without any embarrassment. He put his own clothes and bag into his locker and secured it with his padlock. He didn't trust anyone and didn't want some random snooping at his stuff. Now in his blues, sporting white rubber clogs, he stepped out into the hospital world. He could now play a different character, a person of importance, a person needed by others. He smiled as he walked the hospital corridor, passing physios in their white tunics, doctors in their white coats, ward sisters in navy and nurses in various colours. All busy heading to wards, clinics and appointments, with Richard now part of the team and feeling part of a team. Entering a ground floor lift, he pressed Floor 2, the 'ping' swiftly sounding his arrival. Stepping out, he turned right, sanitised his hands at the wall station and entered the double two-way doors which had the sign 'Theatre Suite' above them.

"Morning, Richard," said a cheery voice coming from a lady wearing a yellow theatre cap and blue scrubs.

"Morning, Barbara," he replied in his monotone voice.

"Big list for you to collect today." She handed him a clipboard containing a patient list.

Ward 15 Ronald Thurman sat at the top of the list. Richard hung the clipboard on a wall hook, put on a blue theatre cap and grabbed a theatre gurney.

"On my way," he replied, heading back to the lifts to start his day as a theatre porter. Not a surgeon, anaesthetist or nurse, he thought, but part of the team. An important part.

# Chapter 5

The afternoon briefings for the enquiry generally started at 4 pm with officers who were able to attend. Jones took little excuse for team members not attending, with only those officers out on enquiries being the ones whose absence was acceptable. He walked in with a customary scowl upon his face, looked around, and took his seat at the top of the room. The room quietened allowing Jones to open the meeting.

"Right, good afternoon, everybody. The enquiry is moving forward with all of your hard work and I really appreciate that. No doubt you have heard today that the guys reviewing the CCTV have located a vital piece of evidence which may, and I mean, may, have given us an image of a potential suspect. I just want to clarify for the purposes of this investigation, from this moment on this unknown male will be referred to as Subject One. He has not been given "Suspect" status but I do consider him to be a 'Person of Interest' to the investigation, Jones halted, looking around the room to ensure that his point had been understood.

Within the enquiry he would only raise a person to suspect status if he clearly believed them to be responsible for or directly connected to the murder of the victim. This would enable him to clearly delineate, in his policy book, his thought processes. It would also reduce complications at court with defence barristers attempting to 'muddy the waters' by claiming that the chief investigator "desperately suspected all persons he spoke to, as he floundered through the investigation." Court was a complicated and predatory process in which to discredit the police and police witnesses seemed to be the prime goal of the defence with little respect held for honesty and truth.

Jones looked at Rachel and nodded, indicating for her to take over.

"OK, guys." She started handing some A4 sheets to her left, "Coming round the room now are three images of Subject One. Two are from a distance and one a bit closer. They have been through the imaging system and been made as clear as we are able. Each sheet is numbered so take a look and at the end of the briefing I want them all back in. Afterwards, anyone who needs a copy will get one. Our subject appears to a white male, indeterminate age, between five foot ten inches and six foot two inches and of slight build. The most noticeable thing about him is the dark coloured coat which has a fur lined hood and labelled 'Rockport' on it. The closer image shows a glint of light just below the hood line on the face."

"Specs?" a voice spoke up in the room.

"Yes, it could be a reflection from the outdoor light," replied Rachel, "or it could be a trick of the light. Don't get too focussed on the subject wearing glasses. It could be a disguise or it could be nothing. This is a great start for us and we need to identify Subject One to either eliminate him from the investigation or to raise his status within the investigation."

Murmurs started around the room as detectives and staff discussed their own views.

Rachel allowed them to for a minute then brought some order.

"OK, OK, save your chatter for after. We'll do the usual round up of the room. Let us know how your enquiries are going, anything significant that we all need to know and any thoughts on the imagery of Subject One."

The room started in its customary clockwise routine with investigators updating the management team and all members getting the opportunity to clarify points. No other ground-breaking discoveries had been made yet. Jones thanked everybody for their input and then provided his direction.

"The next forty-eight hours are going to be focussed on identifying this male. DI Barnes will liaise directly with the source unit (informants) and will allocate tasks to enquiry teams. I'll schedule this in policy but the sort of things that I want are: Who the hell is he? Where in town sells Rockport coats? Have we had any theft of Rockport coats from the shops? Have any burglaries been reported with Rockports missing? Is he a heroin user? Who has the main drug supply at the moment? Inspector Barnes will allocate them all. Remember A, B, C everybody. Lastly, this is our first break and it's an important one. If he gets identified then I get to know straight away. No-one makes a move on him without my authority." With that, Jones stood up with Andy and Rachel, the team briefing concluded, and the room dispersed.

***

Rachel took the stairs down to the first floor where the source unit had an office. It still astounded her to this day that the unit continued to be based within a police station; just another example of the rank and structure ignorance of covert policing. The source unit were plain clothes officers who were responsible for looking after all the aspects of informants, from meeting them and correctly recording the information that they provided, to looking after their welfare and paying them. They worked by a strict set of rules, despite what their colleagues and members of the public may think, to ensure that the safety and integrity of all was protected. Informants were looked upon as a necessary evil. The realities were that police officers asked criminals to take advantage of their established criminal relationships in order to provide information on criminal activity. The informants were paid in cash, should the police take action on the information and if it proved to be accurate. The police officers themselves were taking advantage of the informants by using relationships which they developed with the informants in order to get information from the informant; the officers were paid their monthly wage. Some would argue a moral dichotomy! Unfortunately, some crimes would not be detected without the use of informants, so the police felt morally justified in using them. Rachel knocked on the door, which was always shut and locked, heard a chair pushed back and watched the door open, seeing the friendly face of Stuart the Detective Inspector look around the door.

"Come in, come in, Rachel, sit down," he said in a South Yorkshire accent.

Rachel entered the small office which was sparsely furnished with two desktop computers and two chairs. In a corner sat a small table with a kettle, the makings for tea and coffee thereon.

"Tea or coffee?" Stuart asked, deftly turning off his computer screen as he lifted the kettle, steam wafting from its spout. "Kettle's just boiled."

"Black coffee Stuart please," Rachel smiled. Stuart started making the drinks using his own mug from his desk and after looking at a couple of mugs on the table top, appeared to choose the cleaner of the two. Rachel observed him as he made it. She had quickly learnt that black coffee was the best option when travelling around stations or police offices. It was hard to mess up the making of a cup of black coffee; no risk of gone off milk or the brown lumpy remains scraped vigorously from an ancient sugar bowl. Stuart turned and handed Rachel her coffee and sat down in the remaining chair.

"Right, how can we help? I'm guessing that you are here about the Wellbury murder. Has the job been given an operation name yet?" All major jobs in the police were given an operational name. This ensured clarity for all departments involved in the specific jobs people were referring to, allowed all information or evidence to be correctly recorded under the same title, thereby assisting with paperwork or legal applications, and also ensured that a budget code could be correctly applied. All aspects of the job would incur a financial cost and at some point, an analyst in headquarters would interrogate the financial data for the benefit of the Chief Officer Team. When the job was reviewed by an external officer, which was best practice, finances would also be reviewed. Everything had a cost.

"Op Torrent," replied Rachel. "Yes, I've come down for some help and for you to task your informants, sorry I mean sources." Informants were now referred to within the police as Covert Human Intelligence Sources (CHIS) or in short, sources. *Where would the police be without an acronym?* she thought cynically, *though I suppose it keeps someone in a job thinking them up.*

"So I'm guessing you've been fully briefed with the wider aspects of Torrent." Stuart nodded his head in confirmation and Rachel continued, "I'll email you with a request regarding all we need but for now I have this." Rachel produced a paper copy of the CCTV image of Subject One, handing it to Stuart.

"We need to know who this is," she stated. Stuart looked at the image and frowned at Rachel.

"You can't see his face, Rachel! That's a big ask - he could be anyone!"

"I know," she replied, "but that's what the boss wants. What CAN you do?"

"OK, Rach, I know you've not worked in the 'CHIS world' but this is how it works. All bosses dislike needing to use CHIS unless they need to. Generally, they just see their information as a pain, or just extra work to do on top of everything else. Until," he raised one finger, "a job comes in like this murder. Then they expect everything from the informants but primarily 'Who did it?' In my opinion, sources rarely come up with the golden nugget. They can point us in the right direction, volunteer some ideas and let us know what is being said on the street. They're unlikely to name this guy. They probably don't know. They may give us a snippet for us to develop."

"OK," said Rachel, as Stuart continued.

"Right, at this time I don't intend to show them this photograph, which we could do. I've already tasked them regarding the victim's use of heroin; who is supplying and what they are supplying. How did he get his drugs? I'll get the officers to reinforce those questions and on top of that I'll ask about the coat; who wears one, anyone nicked one etc. I'm sure they'll come back with something and I'll let you know. Is that OK?"

"That's great, Stuart. I'll let the boss know."

"What's it like working for him then?" asked Stuart, smiling.

"He's OK," replied Rachel, "needs dragging into the twenty-first century though." Stuart laughed.

"At least he's competent," he said. "Too many of them at that rank with no idea and no ability, in my opinion. If the public only knew."

Rachel and Stuart sat chewing the fat whilst enjoying their coffee; a welcome stress relief for Rachel.

***

Joe peeled himself from his single bed, in his damp and cold bedsit, watching his breath in clouds exiting his mouth; lying on the floor next to him, a discarded homemade tourniquet, used syringe and bag of citric acid. He picked up the needle and placed it in a plastic yellow sharps bin, yawning as he did so. The flat was crap: the furniture was the landlord's, with some basic bits supplied by the social, single bed and a small sink with a tiny kitchenette, none of it particularly clean. Joe had slept in his clothes in an attempt to keep warm and finding a jumper on the floor, shoved it on for another layer of insulation. He'd had some gear last night and would need to score later today just so he could feel normal. On the kitchen side were a couple of diazepam which he necked to keep the shakes and cramps at bay. Switching the kettle on, he rinsed a used cup in cold water and chucked in a used tea bag - at least it would be something warm to drink. Music was playing from downstairs, Joe's flat being a top floor flat in a terraced building. He walked to the roof Velux, cracking the window and squinting, allowing daylight and a stiff breeze to enter. The Velux blind had stopped working months ago, so when at home, Joe walked around in a permanent twilight haze. The kettle bubbled vigorously, steam puffing from its spout, the automatic off switch no longer working. Joe switched it off at the wall and poured the steaming water over the lifeless tea bag, causing a green vapid tinge and faint aroma of spearmint to materialize in the cup.

*Not even a proper tea bag*, thought Joe, disgustedly, remembering that he had nicked a handful last week whilst passing an outside cafe. Just his luck that mint tea was all he had got! He squeezed the last remnants of life from the bag and tasted the yellow tinged liquid. Better than nothing and with no toothpaste at least the mint would freshen up his breath. Joe always tried to look for the silver linings; it was the only way that he could keep going in his poxy little world. He needed a change of luck and thought he may get one when he started helping Wellbury buy his heroin. Rich, fat boy needing Joe's help after all these years but when it came down to it, he wouldn't give Joe anything extra to help him get by. Fatty had deserved what he'd got.

Picking up one of his two coats from the hook on the door, Joe walked out to the landing and communal toilet, having closed his flat door. The toilet door was open and sitting on there, gouching, was Cathy from flat five, jogging bottoms and knickers round her ankles. Joe looked at her in disgust and walked past, down the communal stairs and out the back door to the rear yard where he peed in a corner, before exiting the gate onto the street. A bracing wind slapped Joe's face as he pulled up the hood on his grey Nike jacket. The flat was situated on the north side of the town with the rear aspect facing the North Sea, thereby taking the

brunt of winds and rains emanating from it. The stiff breeze was regarded as "invigorating" by most, but by a smackhead starting to rattle, it was cold, intrusive and relentless. Joe turned left, heading towards the town. He was due to get his 'script' in twenty minutes at a town centre pharmacy and he didn't want to miss it.

At eleven o'clock, Joe stood with one other at the pharmacy counter waiting to receive his prescribed methadone. The pharmacy had a strict policy for the drug to be taken on site for which they had a screen, secluding a small area of the pharmacy. Joe waited his turn and then approached the counter, was handed a cup containing the clear liquid which he necked in one mouthful. He smiled at the pharmacy assistant who forced a smile back.

"Thanks," said Joe, as he left the pharmacy. Despite the degrading feeling it gave him, receiving his methadone in this fashion, it did no good to be rude to the assistants giving him the drug. They may not realise it but they were a real lifeline to him. The methadone would take about half an hour to start having any effect, when it would hold at bay the side effects of being drug dependent.

Joe checked his phone and saw that the Tommy line was up and running already. He had a tenner left in his pocket so he could afford a bag this morning which meant he'd just have to scrounge some food and drink from in town later on. Tucking into an empty shop doorway he made a call into the line. The phone rang out a couple of times and then was answered.

"Who's dat and what are yer after?" said an anonymous Scouse voice at the other end of the line.

"It's Joe, one bag."

"Graveyard, half twelve," then the line went dead.

The line was manned by someone in Liverpool for most of the day. That person was unknown to the callers, just an anonymous voice who would direct the users where to go and what time to be there. The voice would be the same for a couple of months and then would change, as someone else directed operations. If the voice didn't recognise you, then you probably wouldn't get served. If you were new to town or a new user you would only get served if you were given an introduction by a reliable and known user. This was a tactic put in place to try to prevent undercover police officers from infiltrating the drug gang or to expose 'grasses' who may report back to the police. If a drugs deal was pounced on by the police or the police seized a large amount of drugs there would be a witch hunt in the criminal gang, as to who the 'grass' was. Linking names to people would always give the gang someone to exact violent retribution against, even if that person was an innocent party. County Lines only worked by preying on the vulnerable and on the threat of swift, unremitting violence if things went wrong.

Joe had an hour kicking around town before he was due to score. Tommy, whoever was playing that role today, would probably be ten minutes late or longer; just another little demonstration of who was in charge of the supply. Inevitably, this would mean that in the area, users would be clumped in little servile groups, tucked away in corners, trying not to draw attention to themselves. Joe would turn up early but tended to keep to himself; that way he could scout out the area for cops, as he didn't fancy a trip to the nick. He took a slow wander to the top of town and half an hour later approached a side entrance of the graveyard, which sprawled from its central church in all directions. At this location he could see the front entrance to the graveyard and also a low stone wall which ran adjacent to the main road. Sure enough, two or three users were already sitting on the wall waiting. Houses and flats overlooked the cemetery and Joe assumed that the Scousers would have taken over one of them today so that they had a good view of the area. It was twelve thirty and five more figures approached the front gate entering the cemetery. That would be it, the dealers wouldn't risk any more people together, they'd have arranged another deal for some others in an hour.

Looking left, Joe saw a young blond haired lad enter the cemetery, wearing a grey Adidas tracksuit and baseball cap. He'd seen him before but not for two or three months. This was today's Tommy, as he walked with a cocky bounce in his step with not a care in the world, hands in his pockets. Joe looked around, checking: no sign of the police or of any strangers but still Joe held back. Tommy's punters clocked him and approached in a huddle, tenners at the ready. Quick exchange of drugs and cash and all parted, scattering in different directions, Tommy turning and retracing his route. Joe entered the cemetery, walking a path parallel with him, knowing Tommy would have seen him. The paths converged at a natural junction.

"Now then mate got a cig, I'm Joe."

"Iya fella, this way," he nodded towards some flats. "We need a quick chat about that dead lad."

Joe followed, if he was honest with himself, slightly worried. He had no option but to go. He needed his bag and if he ran from this lot, they'd stop serving him and catch up with him later on down the line. Tommy took him towards a ground floor flat with disabled ramp access. *Evil sods*, Joe thought to himself, *they've taken George's flat again.*

George was a well-known heroin addict in the town who moved around in a wheelchair. He was an amputee and managed to pull and push himself around with his one good leg. Nobody really knew how long he'd been on the gear; he was just one of those who had "always been around" and was probably about fifty years old now. The Scousers had used his flat previously, before being chased off by the police. Now they'd come back, had probably knocked on his door and when he opened it, cuffed him over the head, telling him that they were moving in for a while. George had no choice; he couldn't fight back and besides, he'd get a free bag of smack every now and then. They didn't give a monkey's, just another easy option for them. They'd return time and time again, despite the police, and they knew that George would always let them in. Tommy reached for the intercom on the door, which he buzzed and when answered just said, "Joe and me." The opening buzz sounded and Tommy gestured forward saying, "After you." Joe frowned but stepped forward, pushing against the door he entered. Hair suddenly grabbed from behind, punched in the stomach, he bent double. Head smashed onto a kitchen surface; calling out in fright, as his head was lifted up and smashed down again.

"Ya little divvy," a voice shouted in his ear, the weight of a body holding him down. Joe instinctively tried to shove back, but head spinning, he couldn't move. His face mashed into the unyielding cold surface, his view bizarrely focused upon a McDonald's take out ketchup. Suddenly, yanked backwards by his hair roots, legs swept from under him, he landed backside first in an armchair.

"Don't move," said the male in front of him, who stood holding a kitchen carving knife.

"Hang on, hang on, there's no need for that," mumbled George's croaking voice.

"GET LOST, OLD MAN!" the knife man shouted at George, "turn around and face that wall. Go on. NOW, this has nothing to do with you," he indicated to George who was sitting in his wheelchair. Joe watched George pathetically use his one leg and shuffle the chair to face the wall, an act which he was obviously used to doing when this lot were around. It was a pathetic and sad act to watch.

"Right, Joey," the knife man continued, "we haven't met, but boy we are now. You can call me T." T was a stocky male, with tattoos on neck and forearms the size of Joe's thighs. Hair cropped short, he looked hard as nails, the knife in his hands reinforcing Joe's opinion of him.

"What have I done?" Joe asked, voice trembling.

"SHUT UP!" shouted T threateningly, moving forwards with the knife. "Listen," he said more quietly. Joe sat still, terrified, head pounding and bricking himself.

"We know about the death. He owed us some money and we know that you were scoring for him. That means that he still owes us, or if you've been short-changing us, then you owe us. Either way YOU owe us."

"I didn't, eh don't have..."

Slap... Joe's head rocked to the side as an open hand collided with his face, the sound splitting the air. A single scream of pain; he never saw it coming. Face stinging and uncontrollable tears on his face, his cheek burned, a red imprint forming. Tommy laughed as George's head shrunk into his neck like a timid tortoise.

"You owe us," repeated T menacingly. "That's all there is to it. If you don't want to end up like he did, sort it out."

"How much do you want?" Joe whimpered, now cradling the left side of his face.

"Two hundred. Now get lost. You DO NOT want to meet me again, believe me." T tossed a small, silver wrap at Joe, who retrieved it from his lap. A hand grabbed him roughly by the arm, shoving him towards the door, which was opened by a smiling Tommy.

"See you soon, lad," said Tommy, as Joe was shoved out of the flat, the door slamming behind him.

Joe breathed in the fresh cold air trying to calm himself, his heart still racing. Walking away from the flat, he headed downhill towards the beach and the sea, hands still shaking and head still aching. That was too close, he knew that he shouldn't have got mixed up with Wellbury. Sure, he'd been to his house loads of times; he'd been into the house whilst Wellbury was finding the cash to pay for the drugs. He could have robbed him or even burgled him; he'd done burglary before. He knew that Wellbury had a floor safe, as the arrogant fool had opened it once when he was there. He'd end up the same as Wellbury, thought Joe. *No thanks, you dirty Scouse git. Touch me again and you will, though. You caught me off guard, never again.*

Joe rubbed his cheek, with the sea air making it sting more. Heart and head calming, he started to plan how he was going to get out of this one. He was good at plans; he'd think of a way to get them the money - two hundred was a lot to get them to leave him alone. Think things through thoroughly, plan the details, check them and then act; Matt had taught him that.

Well, he had a wrap of smack. He hadn't paid for that apart from his beating. There was always a silver lining. Joe smiled to himself and continued downhill to the seafront.

# Chapter 6

Matthew walked out of the High Street Waterstones, having had a browse of its shelves and displays, which assisted him in gauging how the competition were doing things. As an independent retailer, he would always struggle with the big book chains and with the superstore's bulk purchasing of best sellers, which they could afford to sell at bargain prices. Matthew's shop relied on local support from customers and in providing a different buying experience than the big retailers. He felt that he had found a niche with local interest and a relaxed friendly environment in which to browse. It didn't do any harm to check other shops out though, and whenever he travelled anywhere in the country, he would seek out a local bookseller for ideas.

He entered Costa and stood in the queue, looking at the display counter, his mind arguing against health, taste or abstinence. The caramel shortbread, on which he considered himself a connoisseur, was probably the best that he had ever eaten, with only The Kitchen in a local village coming close with its gargantuan slice of heaven. Matthew plumped for abstinence and only ordered a caramel latte 'to go'. Having taken a quick break from his shop, he returned with his coffee, unlocked the door and changed the 'closed' sign to 'open'.

Half an hour later, Matthew sat contemplating the fragile existence of life, having finished the last chapter of Anna Karenina whilst sipping on his coffee. Tolstoy's novel was a classic which he had enjoyed but now maybe time for something lighter to read. However, his unconscious mind had clearly been mulling over Rachel's latest case. A murder made to look like a suicide. *Very Agatha Christie,* he thought and smiled.

Matthew found death fascinating and spent many

hours with his head buried within crime thrillers and murder mystery novels, but as a book retailer, he should have a wide knowledge of all genres, hence reading the Tolstoy tome. He looked around the shop, which was currently empty of customers, despite the cold and blustery day outside. Time to choose another book to help him while away the hours, and besides, he had some research to do. The luxury of having his own shop with no boss to shout at him, nobody to tell him what to do; he could while away his hours as he thought fit.

Scanning the shelves, Matthew picked up Andrew Niederman's 'The Devil's Advocate', recognising the film title which he had seen some years ago, the plot centring around a lawyer who successfully defends guilty clients within the law courts. *This will do*, he thought, in what he considered was a bit of light reading. The doorbell to the shop pinged and behind steamed glasses and a face wrap, Matthew recognised Geoff.

"Morning, Geoff," greeted Matthew cheerfully. Geoff raised a hand in greeting whilst loosening his scarf with the other. Glasses removed, he squinted at the shelves in the shop, and wiped them carefully to clean them. Carefully replaced, he moved hesitantly forward to the till area. He always seemed an awkward and shy man to Matthew, with whom he had never really had a prolonged conversation. Matthew presumed him to be retired, based on his age and frequent attendance at the shop, but had no idea what his working career had been; although interested to know, Matthew felt that Geoff may find the question intrusive.

"Morning, sir," said Geoff, in his well-spoken tone, "I'm wondering whether you could order me a copy of Do No Harm by Henry Marsh?"

"I'll certainly give it a go, Geoff. It'll probably take me a bit to research and locate if that's OK?"

"Yes, no problem at all. No rush. Thank you. Good book?" Geoff asked, nodding to Niederman.

"Just getting started on it. I'll let you know," replied Matthew. Geoff smiled and moved to the rear of the shop to browse.

Matthew had written the title down and would check his online systems for the book. He was used to obscure orders from Geoff and would do his best to honour them, as he was a loyal and a good paying customer. Niederman would have to wait for a while and was placed beneath the counter for later in the day.

***

Rachel sat within her office reviewing Jones' policy document when her work mobile rang.

"Hello, DI Barnes speaking."

"Hi boss, it's Tom from one of the enquiry teams."

"Hi Tom, how's things going? What can I do for you?" Rachel replied, thinking how easily it had become to accept being called 'Boss' instead of just Rachel. In all honesty, Rachel didn't care either way but it probably took longer to explain that to anyone, than to just accept what they used.

"All fine thanks. Just thought that I should run something past you," Tom continued. "I've been doing house to house enquiries, concentrating on immediate neighbours. I don't think we knew this but apparently the victim had a cleaner who visited two or three times a week."

"OK," replied Rachel, "I think that's new. Any more detail on him or her?"

"It's a female, Boss. No name yet but I have got a vehicle reg for a little red Corsa. Apparently, she's about thirty-five years old, brunette, quite a fit lass and visited sometimes during the day, sometimes the evening. I'm guessing that she probably has got a set of keys to the house, alarm codes etc," finished Tom.

Rachel raised her eyebrows at 'fit' being used in this context, describing a good looking woman, as she replied, "OK Tom, good work. Let's get that information into the intelligence cell and start seeing who she is. I don't want her approaching until we know a bit about her. Thanks for letting me know. I'll wait for your update when you get back here." Rachel terminated the call. Another person to add into the mix; someone who could add more information to the victim's personal life, but they'd have to tread carefully. There was probably more to this than met the eye; a cleaner who had attended the house daytime and evening with legitimate access; someone who had not contacted the police despite Wellbury's death being splashed all over the papers; somebody with something to hide.

*\*\**

Sheila Wilmslow arrived home in her little red Corsa, parking on the driveway of her small semi-detached house and gave a big sigh. Another day's work was completed in the houses of richer people than herself, but she couldn't complain too much as they paid her wages. She reached to the back passenger windows and removed her advertising signs, which had been stuck to the interior of the windows with small suction cups, displaying her business 'Sheila's Maid – no job too small'. Sheila was the proud owner of her own cleaning company. Well, 'proud' was an overstatement. Sheila worked because she had to. Married at twenty six to a man fifteen years her senior, she had expected to be a housewife, supported by a rich husband, but instead earned her own income by scrubbing floors and cleaning basins. Her husband had always insisted on them having separate finances and for Sheila to support herself. Sure, he'd bought the house outright and his wage paid the bills, he even bought her nice dresses when it suited him, if he had the need for her on his arm at a work function. That was it though; Sheila didn't consider herself to be a kept woman. He'd bought her the car outright and helped her with the basics of setting up the business, then over to her. Her husband worked away every week in London and frequently had prolonged periods of time down in 'The City' as he called it. He had something to do with Human Resources; Sheila wasn't sure what, except to say that he was a high-flying manager of sorts. All Sheila knew for sure was that he owned this house, her car and a very nice flat in the centre of London. The other thing Sheila was sure of was that she was bored of him and had been for some time. She sighed, got out of the car and entered the house.

The three bedroom house was tastefully decorated, its interior decor planned by Sheila. Nothing too flash but with stylish furniture and no kids or pets to ruin it. Sheila kept it clean; her business only employed herself with no extra staff.

"Alexa, music please," stated Sheila in a local Barnston accent, as she wandered to the fridge, where she knew she had a bottle of Sauvignon Blanc waiting. She kicked off her shoes, which skidded across the floor, stopped by a Shaker unit, and removed the bottle from her pastel green Smeg fridge. She'd been drinking a lot recently, her nerves shot to pieces with what had gone on with Frank; who wouldn't be! She was expecting the police to come for her at some point; no doubt some bloody nosey neighbour will have said something about her working for him, though it was none of their business.

She could feel herself winding up, her anger simmering as she thought about it; an anger which she knew she struggled to control. Frank is dead! Found dead in the home she cleaned, found on a night that she'd been there. She took a large slug of wine, anger bubbling, mounting, and they'll link me, all because "THAT EXCUSE OF A HUSBAND IS AWAY AGAIN!" she screamed out loud, stamping her feet on the floor and drumming her fists on the marble kitchen surface, Vesuvius erupting. She wouldn't have been cleaning for him if her husband properly supported her, she wouldn't have gotten involved with Frank if her husband was ever home. She sobbed, mascara tears running down her face as rivulets trailed lines on her powdered cheeks, then silence.

"That's better," she said to herself shaking her head to clear it, now taking a sip from her glass and smiling. "Time for a bath, relax and get changed." Sheila had a date tonight with Sebastian and was looking forward to a wonderful dinner and great company. She wandered from the kitchen smiling; a different woman, heading upstairs listening to the music of Beyonce's 'Irreplaceable'.

The bath now running, Sheila wandered into her room adorned in her Hilton Hotel robe, which she had stolen three years ago on her one and only London trip to visit her husband. She had attended a work dinner with him as his dutiful wife, smiled at the right time, danced when asked to and was "a real hit" according to her husband. She had left the party early and alone though and spent the late part of her evening in the hotel apartment with only a television for company. Leaving the hotel the following day, she packed the robe and took the train back to Fenchurch. 'He' had stayed in London for work. Sheila should have realised what her life would be like then but blinded by dreams and hope, she didn't.

Hearing that the tub was full, Sheila switched off the

tap, disrobed and enjoyed the luxury of a hot bath, a glass of chilled wine and lay back thinking of Sebastian. Ironically, she had been introduced to Sebastian by his own wife who was looking for a cleaner and called Sheila's Maid to get a quote. Sheila attended the Mount Way address to meet Mrs Briggs and whilst touring the house, met Sebastian in his office. Sebastian appeared to give her a cursory glance, though Sheila noted his eyes lingered on her curves, and advised his wife to employ whomever she wished. The quote was supplied and later that day, Sheila was offered the job to start the following week. The work was relatively easy as the family were generally tidy and Sheila found that she could swiftly get the house completed. Mrs Briggs was often out whilst she cleaned but on occasion Sebastian was at home. On those occasions Sheila took her time and secretly enjoyed his attention, spotting him looking at her when he didn't think he could see, a little bit of conversation here and there, she gave particular care to Sebastian's office, especially when he was present. The affair started when Sebastian 'innocently' asked Sheila if he could meet her after he finished work to discuss her employment, suggesting that they meet in a bar on the south side of town. Sheila was not naive and dressed to impress that evening, both drank too much, enjoying a clumsy "snog" when they parted. The first meeting led to others, meals out, nights away, and sex in the family home when Sheila was cleaning. All of this was unfair to Mrs Briggs and her kids but the thrill, the naughtiness of it… it was wrong, but Sheila loved it and besides, she was lonely.

An hour later, Sheila had blow-dried her hair, put on her face and dress and walked from her front door to a waiting taxi, wrapped in a warm black Cashmere coat, clutching her Kurt Geiger Mini Kensington closely. Climbing into the taxi, she directed the driver to take her to Carlucci's, a small quiet restaurant on the south side of Barnston. Taxi paid, she entered the restaurant where her coat was taken and she was directed to the bar where she would wait for Sebastian. He was often late to their secret liaisons, but when you were a partner in a law firm, that could only be expected. Sheila thought his lateness quite reasonable; at least he lived and worked in the town, she saw more of him than her own husband. She ordered a white wine spritzer awaiting his arrival.

***

Sebastian turned off the lights to his offices in the town centre, set the alarm, locked the doors and listened for the familiar alarm tones, indicating that the alarm was set. Pulling his coat collar up, he could smell the Dior aftershave he had just sprayed clinging to the collar. With a bounce to his step and a smile to his face, he headed to Carlucci's; his wife at home with the kids believed him to be working late again. A wife who knew not to ring him if he was going to be late, as he would be with a client, probably in the police station, waiting to guide them through an interview. Sebastian's life was good. An obedient and considerate wife at home, two lovely kids and a gorgeous girlfriend who was desperate to see him at any opportunity she could. With a set of keys for the house, they could take advantage of opportunities anytime that they wished to.

The town was quietening down after the evening rush hour had concluded, the streetlights were on and the familiar biting North Sea air buffeted hats and hairstyles, as pedestrians navigated the streets. The restaurant on the south side was fairly new, with an exquisite menu and an intimate feeling. As usual, Sebastian was careful when going to meet Sheila, not taking the direct route to the restaurant but diverting down some side streets. Waiting at a couple of road ends, just checking that he didn't see anyone he knew or, more importantly, no one saw or recognised him. It was easier in the wintertime, with darkness for cover; cheaper too, with no need to travel away on bogus conferences during summer, just to hide any liaison he had. Sheila hadn't been the only one; in his mind, she was just the current one.

*\*\**

Unbeknown to Sebastian Briggs, he had been seen. He'd been watched locking up his business premises; he'd been watched as he entered the south side of town; he'd been watched as he scampered out of a small side street heading towards the doorway of Carlucci's and entering. Briggs never noticed the cyclist silently gliding beyond him as he entered the restaurant; he'd been looking for cars, looking at pedestrians, and if he had even noticed a push bike, his mind had discounted it as irrelevant. The cyclist walked back towards the restaurant and looked in the large front window, seeing Briggs greet a smartly dressed lady, who was sitting at the bar, with a tight cuddle and a kiss. Obviously, more than just friends and clearly not Mrs Briggs: this was another of Briggs' conquests. The cyclist knew Mrs Briggs by sight from seeing her at the family home. They also knew this lady; they had seen her there too, exiting the red Corsa with the Sheila's Maid logo on it, another victim of Briggs' adulterous attention.

*\*\**

Stuart's telephone rang, it was ten thirty at night, and

he answered.

"Hi Dave, is everything OK?"

"Yes, Stu," replied Dave, one of the detectives who worked for Stuart. "One of the sources has been in contact and wants a meeting tomorrow. They've got something for us in relation to the murder."

"OK, give them a call back and arrange a meeting. I'll be coming with you. Make it for around ten so I can clear up some paperwork in the office."

"Will do, see you in the morning," replied Dave and terminated the call.

*At last*, thought Stuart, *one of them has got back with something*. It was nothing to get excited about though. Stuart had learnt over a number of years not to get too excited with these calls, as the source's belief of a really good bit of information was not always what the police believed would be of interest. Well, he'd see what tomorrow would bring; he had a busy day anyway so another meeting thrown in would only add to it. Turning out the lights in his flat, he headed to bed, phone in hand: he was on call so had to be prepared to take any calls that came in overnight. Oh, the joys of being a police officer.

# Chapter 7

The following morning at 7 am, Stuart swiped his warrant card against the digital lock of his office and entered its sparse surroundings. He had a lot of work to do today making sure that all his staff were gainfully employed, that all relevant intelligence was recorded correctly and that his officers had planned any meetings they had meticulously. It was Stuart's job to make sure that the wheel didn't come off for his team or the organisation. Working with informants was a dangerous occupation in the police and the integrity of the system had to be maintained at all times. Sources, by their very nature, tended to live chaotic lifestyles, living on the edge of the criminal world or indeed within it. It was Stuart's team's responsibility to add some calm to the chaos, to work within the laws and prescribed rules and to ensure that they maintained safety for themselves, the organisation and the source. Every action and meeting was documented clearly and intelligence disseminated appropriately. Stuart managed the whole team and like many managers within the police service, was chained to a desk for most of the day. Sticking the kettle on and fixing a coffee, he also kicked his computer into life, letting it run through its various security protocols, sounds emitting from the email system, advising him of management meetings, reports to be completed and information requests. The email system itself was enough to swamp a small town; people had forgotten how to talk to each other in Stuart's opinion. Not his team though, that's what they were paid to do: speak to the sources in a way they both understood and come back with information, leaving both parties happy. Some of his detectives wouldn't last two minutes speaking with senior managers, trying to decipher the organisational jargon and work out the interminable initialisms and acronyms. They wouldn't want to; they were real police officers doing real jobs. An hour later, having waded his way through some emails by reply or delete, there was a knock on Stuart's door, which he opened.

"We're all in, Stu," said Dave, nodding to the adjoining office. The meeting is scheduled for ten in Fenchurch."

"OK mate, cheers," said Stuart, grabbing his third coffee of the day, following Dave into the team office. "Morning all," said Stuart on entering.

This office, too, was sparsely furnished with no paperwork lying about, complying with the clear desk policy, which was part of the standards of the office. Stuart looked around the team which comprised Dave, Helen and Jim; each officer good in their own ways but all different characters. Dave looked a mess with wavy shoulder length hair and a scruffy beard, he fitted in at most places and could talk to anyone. Helen was skinny as a rake with long brown hair; when she chose to, she could either look like she'd been dragged off the street or just walked out of the fanciest hotel. Jim… well Jim, was mind-numbingly boring but he was a crack on the computer and his attention to detail was terrific. He was the safety net for the other two, and for Stuart too if he was honest. Bald as a coot, Jim could blend in anywhere and if a distraction was required, then his superlative knowledge of the formation of the railways throughout Northern England, was enough to make any inquisitive member of the public 'do a Lord Lucan'. Stuart had a good team at the moment and he knew it.

"Right guys, I'm sure Dave will have given you the update from last night, so we all have a meeting to cover today. Over to you, Dave."

Dave then again covered the short conversation he had

with the source the previous evening and the team discussed how and where the meeting would be held. All meetings were planned by the team as a whole; four brains were better than one, thereby limiting any chance of compromise to the team or the source.

"Right Dave, so the tickets have been bought and put in the safe box?" asked Stuart.

"Yes boss, the source will collect them and we'll meet them at Fenchurch."

"OK then, let's get going. We'll take two cars across there. Helen and Dave will do the meeting with Jim and me in support. Is everyone happy that they know what their role is?" Stuart received nodded assent from the team. "OK, see you across there." Stuart exited the team office, returning to his own where he switched off his computer, grabbed his coat, secured his door and met Jim in the corridor outside.

"OK Jimbo, let's get to the car."

*** 

One hour later, the team were in Fenchurch, doing their last minute checks for the meeting. Today the meeting would be held in a public location. Neither the officers nor source were known in Fenchurch, so this would be a safe location to meet. They had chosen a large Costa cafe in the middle of the town which afforded good views. Helen was already inside, with Dave outside waiting to meet the source. Stuart would give him the heads up that she was on her way. She was due to travel from Barnston this morning and used the pseudonym of 'Beth'. Stuart was at the station and would inform her of the meeting location when she arrived at Fenchurch.

At nine forty-five, Dave's phone vibrated in his pocket.

"She's leaving the station now mate and only two others exited the train, both commuters in suits. I've rung her and told her the meeting location; she understands where it is and she's actually tidied herself up! She's wearing blue jeans, a black jacket and a black beret. The meet location will be fine. She sounds nervous though, so treat her gently."

"Cheers Stu, speak to you again in a while."

Dave terminated the call. Looking into the cafe, where Helen was reading a paper, he caught her eye and nodded. She would understand that the meeting was on. This was always the most nervous part of the meeting: waiting for the arrival. Beth was no idiot and would do what she needed to do, to ensure that she wasn't followed by anybody. The officers knew that the location was currently safe and Jim was prepared to step in with a diversion if required.

Looking up, Dave saw Beth approaching with a big smile on her face. He smiled back and they greeted each other as if they were old friends. The first act had commenced. Any onlooker would just see friends meeting for a coffee and would have no idea about the real purposes of the meeting. Officers and sources would play their parts, all understanding the danger which they would be in, should anyone discover that Beth was speaking to the police. Dave bought the coffees and they went to sit with Helen, everyone knowing each other, no need for introductions.

Beth was a normal looking woman in her mid-twenties. She had a thin build and not a great complexion and looked older than her years. Her years of heroin abuse had not been kind to her and aged her beyond her years. Four months previously, she had been brought in for a drug search at the police station. During the search, a Fossil wristwatch had been found on her wrist and on research it transpired that it could have come from a house which had been burgled in Barnston. She was subsequently arrested for the burglary and was now on police bail whilst the offence was fully investigated. The detective in the case didn't believe her to be the perpetrator and it was more likely that she had just been given the watch, but with a "no reply" interview, recommended by Briggs who represented her, Beth had admitted nothing. She had now been working for the police for a couple of months in the desperate hope that they would make the investigation go away. The reality was that Dave couldn't do that for her. The only thing that he could do was to encourage her to be honest in the investigation and if she was charged with any offence, provide the magistrate or judge with a letter advising them of her assistance provided to the police. Beth had advised Dave that she hadn't burgled anybody's house and had found the watch lying in one of the flats within her building block and had taken it. No one had said anything, so she'd kept it. Whether that was true or not, Dave didn't know; they'd see how the investigation panned out and meanwhile get as much information from Beth as they could.

The meeting started with Dave checking on Beth's welfare: doctor appointments, methadone script and her current drugs misuse. Then straight to the point.

"So Beth, what have you got for us?" asked Dave, preparing to make brief notes on Helen's newspaper, as Helen kept an eye on the door and the surrounding customers.

"The Scousers are back on again. Here's their current number," she passed a small piece of paper over. "They still keep changing places where they deal from. It was the North graveyard yesterday."

"How do you know that?"

"Me friend rang and scored from them yesterday. I was with her when she went but I'm trying to stay off it." Beth smiled; she knew how to play this game. Tell the coppers what they needed and lie about her personal drug misuse. What they didn't know wouldn't hurt them and besides, she liked Dave; he was normal, just a shame he was a cop.

"I've heard they've moved in with that one-legged bloke again."

"George?"

"Yeah, that's him. Poor sod's terrified of them."

"How long they been there then?"

"About three days?"

Dave looked at Beth. *And of course, your friend has scored from them for three days and not you*, he thought to himself. *Likely story*. Dave was no-one's fool either but just smiled at Beth and continued.

"What else?"

"That Joe that lives in my block was getting Fatty's drugs for him. He was getting it from the Scousers." Dave's ears pricked up: this is what he'd come to hear. He kept his face calm.

"Who is Joe?"

"I dunno his other name, just Joe. He lives on the same floor as me and is obviously a smackhead. He's a local, bit of a cocky git." Dave got Joe's description which would, combined with the flat location, be enough to identify him.

"Who do you mean by Fatty?"

"That Wellbury bloke. The one that's been found dead at home. He's all over the papers."

"So tell me why you think Joe was getting him drugs?"

"Well," Beth started, sipping her coffee and enjoying the attention, "I got off me head with him about two

83

months ago. He was trying to get in me knickers when I was sharing his gear. He said that he was loaded at the moment cos he was keeping Fatty right with the Scousers. Two and two together, you see," she finished, winking at Dave. She looked over at Helen, giving her a brief smile. Dave continued with his notes.

"So have you been in Joe's flat?"

"Yeah, of course"

"Describe it to me?" Beth described the flat layout, furniture etc, it didn't take long.

"What's Joe generally wear then? You know, when he's out and about?" continued Dave.

"Same old crap as the rest of us. Trackies or joggers, trainers."

"It's Baltic out there at the moment," continued Dave, "any hats or coats?"

"Course he wears a coat, you daft git. He's like me, no meat on his bones."

"What coat's he wear? If I saw him on the street, would I know him?"

"Probs not," Beth replied. "Coats, coats..." she pondered. "I think he's got a grey Umbro or Nike, something like that." Dave felt a bit deflated, but at least he had the victim's potential drug supplier to stick into the investigation.

"Oh yeah, and he's got a dark coloured Rockport with a fur lined hood," Beth finished.

Dave's eyes flicked to Helen. *Jackpot*, he thought to himself, his facial expression not changing, his insides twisting with exhilaration.

The meeting continued for five more minutes with Dave probing for more detail but they had what they needed. Helen, David, and Beth stood up simultaneously and headed for the door. Exiting, they said their goodbyes with Beth returning to the station and Helen and Dave in the direction of their parked car.

Five minutes after they left Costa, Jim, wearing a dark suit, terminated his phone call, closed his Apple Mac, put on his dark grey gabardine coat and walked out of the cafe too. He then strode away to meet with Stuart to drive back to the office.

***

The team walked back into their office to debrief the morning's meeting. Dave took the lead, covering the welfare issues and then went on to describe the details regarding Joe, the victim and the Rockport coat.

"Great work," said Stuart, smiling. Jim was already tapping on the computer keyboard, researching the information that Beth had provided. An address, first name and description should make his identification easy work with a research of the intelligence system. Sure enough, within two or three minutes, "Here's your man," said Jim out loud. The team crowded around his computer trying to get a look at the details.

"Joe Marsden, lives at Chandler's Terrace in a multi-occupancy building; a heroin user with previous for theft, handling stolen goods and burglary." Staring out from the screen was a police photograph of Joe, smiling at the camera, taken the last time that he was in police custody.

"That smile will soon be wiped off your face, son," said Stuart, looking at the photograph. "Let's get the intelligence on the system and get it sanitised. I'll check it before we release it. I'm going to pass this one verbally to DI Barnes when I can find her. Good work team, great work." Stuart left the office in search of Rachel.

Rachel was in the nick and when called by Stuart, walked down to his office. The door was ajar and she knocked and walked in. Waiting for her, Stuart had two coffees on the desk, then closed the door behind her.

"Well, we've come up with something, Rach. It could give you a line of investigation."

"OK."

"The name I have been given is Joe Marsden," said Stuart, turning his screen around and showing Rachel his police intelligence profile. "It's from a reliable source but the information, which will be disseminated, is that he supplied drugs to Wellbury and a clothing description of his usual attire, including the Rockport coat." Stuart then explained to Rachel the full details of the information supplied to him. Rachel knew better than to ask who the source was.

"This doesn't mean that Marsden is our murderer," Stuart stressed. "All we are saying is that he owns the coat and that he has previously supplied your victim with heroin. It's a starter for ten and up to you and the boss how you want to play it. The intelligence will be on the system in half an hour for the investigation team's eyes only at this time."

"Nice one, Stuart. That's given us two persons of interest now. I'll speak to the boss and we'll make some decisions at this afternoon's briefing.

***

Another early shift completed at work, Richard sat on the train returning to Barnston, tired out after a day of lifting patients on and off theatre trolleys for the various procedures which they had undergone. He'd dumped his used scrubs in the gurney at work and grabbed a clean set to bring home. You weren't supposed to but they'd come in for something. He enjoyed the views from the window and the gentle roll as the train sped along. Tomorrow was due to be a day off for him but he was also on the bank of porters to work occasionally at Barnston Hospital, so he had a shift there tomorrow; the extra money would come in handy. The train started its run into Barnston and Richard stood up, grabbed his bag and prepared to get off at the station, waiting for the green light on the door to illuminate once the train had stopped. The platform seemed fairly empty with only four or five people waiting to board. The train stopped and with the light now illuminated, Richard opened the door and jumped out onto the cold platform heading for the exit. Walking out of the station and heading to Waterstones, he spotted Joe Marsden walking in the direction of a bookie, no doubt to keep warm.

Change of coat for you, Joe boy, thought Richard to himself, making a mental note of it. Richard continued walking and on entering Waterstones, was welcomed by the temperate air produced by the overhead heat pump. He headed for the crime thriller section, checking alphabetically for the letter N. There it was and there he was; Andrew Niederman's 'The Devil's Advocate'. He'd read about this book on the internet: it looked a good read and was exactly what he was after. Paying for it in cash, he then left the shop and zipping up his coat, watched Sebastian Briggs locking up for the day at his business address before he strode off in his expensive suit, to fleece some more of the public's money defending guilty criminals. The thought angered Richard, who lived in his crappy little flat, working extra shifts to get by whilst the Sebastians of this world lived in luxury. He turned away in disgust, heading towards Tesco's, where he'd grab a ready meal to cook in his microwave and spend the evening reading.

*\*\**

Matthew locked up his shop after a quiet day at work and walked through the precinct to the top of town where he parked his car for the day. Very little custom today; it appeared that the town had been quiet all round. He hadn't run today so intended to do so when he got home, before tea, and before Rachel got home. Looking up, Matthew saw Richard Greaves crossing over the precinct from the direction of Waterstones, walking beyond the law firm where Briggs the solicitor had just left. Greaves had a look of hatred on his face before turning the corner left, away from view.

*Maybe not so loyal after all*, thought Matthew, turning right towards his car park. He walked up to his Volkswagen Golf and headed home.

*** 

Four o'clock at Barnston Police Station and the team sat in the briefing room, ready to start. Detective Superintendent Jones had been writing policy all afternoon, having spoken with Rachel and continued to write it in the office next door whilst Rachel headed the briefing. Rachel had commenced the briefing by going around the room checking the updates from each team of officers. CCTV had now continued to develop with evidence of a red Corsa arriving at the house during the evening, a woman exiting the vehicle and entering the house and at 9 pm the same woman exiting and leaving the address in the car. Local CCTV in the area had so far failed to find the Corsa leaving the street or indeed the south side area. Toxicology results had now returned on the victim, showing a high dose of heroin within the sample, indicative of an overdose. Contact had been made with the victim's only other known next of kin, an uncle who had been living in Australia for some time and had not spoken to the victim in years. The deputy manager of the victim's business interests knew little of his private life and was concentrating on the day to day management of the business but would "help in any way he could with the investigation." House to house enquiries to date had revealed nothing new to progress the investigation.

"OK everybody, thanks for those updates," said Rachel. "Mr Jones has been writing policy decisions all afternoon and is still doing so next door. They'll be typed up this afternoon and available for you all to read. There will be some clear definite lines of enquiry, following an update I will give you, and some direction to progress the investigation." Rachel looked around the room, ensuring that she had everyone's attention. "Today, I have received some accurate and reliable intelligence that a male by the name of Joe Marsden of Chandlers Terrace has been responsible for the supply of heroin to the victim." A photograph of Marsden was displayed on the smart board behind Rachel. Murmurs started in the room. Rachel raised her voice slightly.

"Quiet please." The room went silent. "Further to this, accurate and reliable intelligence indicates that Marsden is the owner of a dark coloured Rockport coat." The room erupted.

"Yes," one voice.

"We've got him," a couple of other people.

"Get him nicked," from many.

"Quiet, quiet," Rachel again raised her voice and lifted her hands in an attempt to quell the noise.

"This is a very sensitive stage of the briefing and the enquiry. Voices down. Let's not get ahead of ourselves." Again, people calmed, discipline reasserting itself, but the atmosphere in the room was buoyant. They had someone to go at, someone to go after, a possible suspect. Rachel continued.

"Before any questions, I'd just like to make you aware of the policy decisions and actions to be undertaken," Rachel paused. "At this stage Joe Marsden and Sheila Wilmslow will be designated as persons of interest to this enquiry." Voices muttered but silenced when Rachel raised a hand.

"For the following reasons: Wilmslow is believed to be a cleaner for the victim but it is unclear if she had any other type of relationship with the victim. CCTV identifies her car and herself to be at the victim's house on the night in question and at this time her actions post 9 pm are unaccounted for. It is not known why she has not willingly come forward to assist with enquiries. The priority with her is to locate and request a voluntary interview to account for her actions on the night and to determine her relationship with the victim." Rachel had already spoken with the enquiry Actions Manager, who had informed her of the detectives to undertake this enquiry.

"Marsden has been named as a possible supplier of heroin to the victim. He is believed to be the owner of a dark Rockport coat, which could be a match for the coat on CCTV on the night in question. The CCTV indicates that 'Rockport' was given legitimate access to the house that night. Rockport's exit from the house or actions within the house that night are not yet known. Although known to the police for theft and historical burglary, little else is known about him. Intelligence indicates that he sources his heroin from the Scousers who are back in town. We need to recognise that the Scousers are an unknown quantity within the enquiry. Did they know the victim? What is their involvement, if any, in his murder? With all this in mind, we don't know enough about Marsden either. In order to fill some gaps, the boss,"

Rachel nodded towards Jones' office, " has made the decision to place Marsden under surveillance. Andy Burrows will develop that side. Any questions?"

The team spent the next half hour asking and answering questions and discussing the case before Rachel wound up the briefing. Jones would now discuss his decisions with Gold Command (Assistant Chief Constable, Detective Chief Constable or indeed the Chief), who would no doubt ratify his decision and make available resources for the enquiry.

Another day complete with some progress, Rachel was tired but satisfied. The enquiry needed to maintain momentum if they were going to catch and convict their killer. Rachel knocked and stuck her head around Jones' door; he was clearly on the phone to Gold. He raised a hand and gave a thumbs up, Rachel reciprocated with her hand and headed off home.

# Chapter 8

## December 2015

Wellbury's hardware store was situated away from the main precinct shopping area on a busy side road within the town. The store had been established for a number of years and supplied all the items that any household could need. The Wellbury family also owned two small newsagents which also supplied groceries, one situated in the north and one in the south of Barnston, servicing housing estates on either side of the town. The businesses were built through the years by Mr and Mrs Wellbury with the intention of passing them on to their only son Frank when he had completed his education. Frank had grown up assisting at all the stores whilst he learnt his trade, eventually taking over the general management of all the stores when his parents died. The businesses afforded him a good income and with a strong manager at each shop he was able to do little, except to enjoy the profits of his parents' hard won earnings. Despite enjoying the luxuries, Frank had never found himself to be particularly happy, had never settled down, or ever found a partner whom he wanted to settle down with. Frank loved women but despite his affluent lifestyle, had never found the right one for him. They always enjoyed the meals out and trips away but never really engaged with him and his personality. In Frank's mind, he should be the most important in their lives and if they couldn't see that, then what good were they to him? He'd had relationships with a couple of his staff over the years but again they weren't anything special, just disposable items. Once the relationship had run its course, he could arrange for them to be sacked and then he wouldn't have to see them again and be reminded of their inadequacies.

Although successful professionally, Frank's personal life was not great and he knew it. He'd tried spicing it up a bit with alcohol and smoking a bit of weed to no avail; even tried a couple of prostitutes, after all he could afford it, but no joy. Then by chance he'd bumped into Joe Marsden. Well, bumped was not quite correct; Marsden had been caught shoplifting in the hardware store by Frank, who was doing a weekly visit.

## September 2015

Joe had been watching outside of the store, assessing the customers and staff for about twenty minutes now, checking to see whether this would be a good time to enter and do some graft. The shop had been fairly busy and now that it was lunch time, there would be some of the staff on a break; at least two had walked out of the door and into town. That should leave two others inside and there was no security guard on here - Fatty would never pay for one. He checked up and down the road for cops and decided to enter. The store was large, with the till to the left side of the door, the shop floor spreading to the right and towards the rear. Security cameras covered the till, front door and rear door, which Joe knew from entering the shop a couple of days ago for a recce.

Joe dropped the hood down on his Rockport, entered and gave the two female staff members at the counter a smile, as he wandered towards the power tool section of the store. He'd had an order for some drill bits, circular saw blades and jigsaw blades from one of the lads on an estate so this should be an easy touch for him. A couple of customers wandered in the aisles browsing for goods. Joe heard the entrance bell ring as someone else entered; he paid little attention; his eyes now focussed on his target. Moving to the drill sets and tools he picked up a power drill in one hand as he slipped some bits into his inside coat pocket, looking like he was just examining the drill. He checked out a couple of brands then moved to circular saws, picking one up in a similar process.

"Hi there, Joe, isn't it?" said a male voice which came from behind him.

He turned around to be confronted by a male wearing spectacles, with a face he thought he should recognise but couldn't. The male frowned at him.

"It's Richard. We used to go to school together. Richard Greaves."

"Ah! Yes mate, recognise you now," said Joe, smiling, still holding the circular saw and thinking, *go away, this couldn't be a worse time.*

"You're the lad who used to get some crap off Fatty. What a nob he was, eh?" continued Joe.

"He certainly was," sounded a deep resonant voice as a hand clamped on Joe's shoulder. Joe jumped and looking round, was confronted by Fatty Wellbury, who held on to him.

"What are you doing here, Marsden? You buying that or lifting it?" Joe dropped the machine on the floor like a hot potato. Surprised twice in the space of a minute; he must be losing his touch.

"No, no Frank, was just looking at buying it."

"Frank is it now?" sneered Wellbury, "and who's your little helper? Bugger me, it's Greaves," smiled Frank. "Haven't seen you in years." He feinted towards Richard, who jumped back with a squeal. Frank laughed.

"Nothing changes, still a scared little boy." Frank leaned forward menacingly to Richard.

"Get out of my shop and don't come in here again, little boy." Richard turned, unable to stop himself, sick with himself. It was inbuilt in him and he hated himself for it, he hated Wellbury for it, but like a naughty child, he scampered from the shop. Turning his head, as he did so, he caught a glance of Wellbury escorting Joe to his office at the rear of the store.

Frank opened his office door, pushing Joe through first, entered himself and shut the door behind him, blocking the exit with his sizeable body.

"Right, Marsden, I think you and I need to have a chat about the damage you've just caused to my property. Obviously, you had no intention of buying it so I can only assume that you were going to nick it. You've got a reputation around the shops, so I'm guessing the police would be interested in this little theft. Anything else you've got on you before I ring them?"

Joe knew he was knackered. Caught red handed by Fatty in his own shop. How could he talk his way out of this one?

"Frank, look I'm really sorry. I'm on me arse at the moment and was desperate. Don't call the cops on me, it'll just cause you and me hassle."

"Anything else on you?" repeated Frank, moving forwards.

"OK, OK, I got these." Joe reached in his pocket, pulling out the drill bits and blades, not noticing as he did so a small cellophane bag containing foil wraps falling from his pocket to the floor; Frank did though. "Take them back Frank, they're yours anyway," said Joe pleadingly, indicating to the tool parts.

"I will," said Frank, moving swiftly forwards and in the process scooping the bag from the floor. "And in here?" asked Frank, knowing the likely answer.

*Damn*, thought Joe, his heart sinking. Frank was holding his heroin.

"Just a bit of brown, mine Frank, just a bit of personal that I use to chill."

"I'll have that too," smiled Frank, feeling very pleased with himself.

"This is what we are going to do, Marsden. I am going to have a long think about what I am going to do with you. You've damaged a fifty quid saw, which you now owe me for. Your prints are on the bits and blades and I have your drugs. In my eyes that means that you owe me if I don't call the police." Joe tried to intercede but was stopped by Frank's raised hands. "So, on Sunday, that's in four days, you are going to meet me on the South Cliff at the monument and if you do, I'll have a job I need doing and you'll get your drugs back. Understand?"

"Understand," Joe nodded, slightly bewildered at Fatty's play at being Al Capone, but if that's how he wanted it, at least Joe would be walking away scot-free today. Frank turned, opened the office door and gestured with a nod to Joe, "Now bugger off. You'd better be there."

Joe nearly ran out of the office, straight to the front door and left.

Frank laughed to himself; he'd really enjoyed that. He had no idea what he'd get Joe to do or if he'd even turn up but it was a bit of fun. Frank had never tried heroin before but there was a first time for everything and life was too short not to try something once.

Later that night, after a bit of research, Frank tooted heroin for the first time. The initial nausea subsided as a feeling of relaxation hit him and the drug took effect; a numbness enveloped his mind and a calmness descended upon him. The next two nights were the same and Sunday morning. He knew what he wanted from Joe by Sunday and the answer was MORE. Frank had found something to satiate him, never realising that in the next few months, it would be the death of him.

## January 2016

Andy Burrows entered the intelligence office at 8 am to start work. This morning he had a meeting with the Authorising Officer to talk through the surveillance operation to be conducted on Marsden. Members of the public thought that the police could just go out with a surveillance team and follow any people that they wished to in their endeavour to evidence criminality. This could not be further than the truth. A lot of planning had to go into a surveillance operation, the most important being an authorised application, allowing the police to conduct covert observations. All of the guidance was published under the Regulatory Investigative Powers Act (RIPA) with which the police, or any public body, had to comply. Andy would spend his morning ensuring that the paperwork was correct and liaising with the surveillance team.

\*\*\*

Within his office, the surveillance team sergeant John had received the intelligence package on Operation Torrent and his subject for surveillance. The package contained all the information which he required to plan an operation and would help one of his operatives complete an operational order. John walked into the team office and looked at his misfits, choosing who would get this one to plan.

What a sorry lot, he thought to himself, smiling, only sorry to bosses out there who didn't really understand surveillance, of which there were many. Promotion didn't come easily to any officer who decided to dedicate themselves to the covert side of policing, generally thought as a shady area by most in the service. Certainly, none of this lot would be considered, with their long hair, questionable facial hair, coarse language, scruffy clothing, jeans, skirts and all. A happy bunch, but a bunch that the rank was not happy spending time with, let's face it, they may 'catch something'. The only thing that the rank was likely to catch was a good dose of common sense and some new expletives, which they could use at the next management meeting. John liked this work though, he liked his team, he liked being out working amongst the public and he liked following criminals who didn't know he was there. The team's job was to gather intelligence and evidence in relation to criminality to assist police investigations.

"Morning all, we've got another job to plan. This one's Op Torrent the enquiry into the murder of Frank Wellbury. We have a subject and the RIPA should be authorised by lunch time. I want us ready to brief by 11 am and hopefully we will be on the ground by one. Ring your wives, husbands and partners if you need to, as we will be off late." A groan rose from the team which John ignored. They knew the score. If you want regular hours, then don't join the surveillance team. Criminals didn't all work Monday nine till five, so a surveillance team couldn't either. Shift deviations and long days were a norm on the team; worth it if they nailed some vital evidence. John allocated the planning and left the team to it whilst he spoke with the intelligence unit and the enquiry team.

***

Rachel walked into the intelligence cell office at eleven o'clock.

"How's things going, Andy?" she asked.

"Not so good, Rach. The bureau has knocked back the application a couple of times already; not happy with some of the wording, getting us to add more justification to the proportionality. We missed our time slot this morning with the Authorising Officer, so now they aren't free until four this afternoon, when they also want a personal briefing from both of us. They've also stipulated that the application has to go to them, so we can't even bounce it through a different Superintendent."

"Bloody bureau," Rachel replied.

The Authorities Bureau, the 'gatekeepers' for all covert applications within the force, were a small team responsible for ensuring that all activity that the police may wish to conduct was within the law, correctly applied for and correctly authorised. They were there to ensure that everything was done correctly. Although painful at times, Rachel fully understood the need for them; no one wanted to lose a case because they'd failed to get the process right. The bureau scrutinised all operations, putting the applications through their stringent processes, to ensure that the action to be undertaken was necessary, justifiable and proportionate. Defence barristers at court would rip the force to pieces if they got the initial applications wrong, which could mean a whole case folded and a criminal could walk free. She certainly didn't want that.

"When are we going to get the surveillance team out then?" she asked.

"Well, they could go out tonight, but I'd recommend that they start early tomorrow and work a long day. If they get behind him tomorrow and things are going well, then they may have a few long days ahead of them. We can rest them tonight and have them on plot at 7 am. That way, we can guarantee that the authority is in place and all the assessments that we have to do are completed."

"OK, I'll let the boss know and see you later to meet the Authorising Officer."

Andy replied with a raised hand as he picked up a ringing telephone.

***

Richard strolled up to the front entrance of Barnston General Hospital where he was going to be working a shift today. The hospital was a mixture of new and old buildings and serviced the local town as well as the surrounding rural community. As with all hospitals, there was always a shortage of staff in all areas of work. He wasn't well known as a member of staff here but had placed his name lanyard on, so could really wander around the hospital at will. He walked to the staff changing area, put the required code into the security lock and entered. The set up here was similar to Fenchurch's though Richard didn't have a permanent locker here. There were some temporary lockers for bank staff, so his gear could be placed in there. Changed into his scrubs, Richard walked the main corridor when he heard an emergency buzzer sound to his right. A white coated male knocked his shoulder, saying, "Sorry, on call. Crash!" heading through an outpatient door to the right. Richard followed, caught in the moment, presuming the man to be a doctor. *A bit of excitement*, thought Richard, grinning stupidly.

A 'crash' meant that someone had collapsed with a suspected heart attack and the on-call team would come careening from all areas of the hospital to try and stabilise them and save their life. Richard wanted to be part of this. Heading through the door, Richard saw a rotund nurse heading into the patient waiting area where a male had collapsed backwards, still holding his Zimmer frame.

His face was pale and blue lips struggled to pull air into his lungs. An old couple stood nearby, watching with fear as a receptionist led them away. The doctor took the frame and put it to one side as he started chest compressions, and the nurse called for a trolley. Seeing it to his side Richard grabbed the crash trolley taking it to the nurse.

"Tracy, take over compressions." The nurse took over.

"You, the defib pads." Richard was instructed as the doctor ripped the man's shirt open. He passed them and grabbed an Ambu bag (a bag and mouthguard used to assist breathing). Richard knelt down at the man's head, placed it over his mouth and squeezed air into his lungs. Pads on, the doctor checked the screen.

"Asystole," he said out loud, indicating the most serious form of cardiac arrest. "Keep going." Richard heard the buzz of the defib machine as it charged. Paddles in hand and rubbing them together, the doctor said loudly, "Stand back." Tracy and Richard released the patient as the paddles descended, sending an arc of electricity through the male, causing him to jerk stiffly.

*This is bloody great*, thought Richard, trying not to manically grin. *Someone's life in my hands with me in the thick of it; Richard, part of the team. Save him or not; who bloody knows? What a thrill.*

A doctor and two more nurses rushed in, one nurse taking over compressions, the other picking up an adrenaline syringe, the doctor immediately trying to find a vein. A male in scrubs turned and looked at Richard confusedly.

"You a doctor?"

"Hospital porter," replied Richard, grinning.

"Out of my way, then, I'm an anaesthetist," replied the male in scrubs, virtually barging Richard out of the way. Richard tumbled to one side, unnoticed by anyone else, as the anaesthetist grabbed a laryngoscope trying to open the male's airway. *Jerk*, thought Richard, picking himself up, his moment of joy deflated to nothing, as if he was nothing. A great start to his shift, ruined by a smart arsed anaesthetist. He turned in disgust. "Hope the poor old fossil dies," he mumbled as he walked away towards the hospital theatre floor.

*****

Joe stood in his flat looking out of his netted window, onto the street below, as a small blue Peugeot pulled up outside of a hotel premises, situated overlooking the sea. The vehicle sat stationary, lights on, clearly occupied, when after five minutes a female stepped out of the driver's side and a male out of the passenger side.

"Plod," Joe laughed to himself. Stood out a mile when you knew what to look for. With the same stance, the same walk and an air of arrogance, which he could discern even at this distance. Poor gits, but someone had to do their job. They were certainly earning more than he was. What were they up to round here though? Joe had left the room light off, so when the male looked up at Joe's building he didn't flinch, as he wouldn't be silhouetted. Both male and female walked towards the hotel and entered. Joe kept at the window and *There*, two or three minutes later a light came on in a top floor hotel room and silhouetted three people. *Two cops and a member of staff*, thought Joe, *now what are you up to?* The curtain in the room pulled back as Joe watched a head pop quickly forward and back.

"Bloody buffoons have not got a bloody clue," he said to himself. Ten minutes later the male and female left, got back in the Peugeot and drove off. Joe necked a couple of vali's and lay on his bed to chill. Another day of graft tomorrow, he was tired and needed some rest.

# Chapter 9

The surveillance team set off to Barnston from their office using various modes of transport. John had received a call from Rachel at around seven the previous night, advising him that the surveillance was now authorised and could commence as soon as they were able. He'd already arranged for the team to come in early so that they could have a briefing before setting off. Briefing completed, they were now on their way. The intelligence indicated that the subject of the day would be at home, so they would try to follow him from there and see how the day went. Although surveillance was routine for the team, starting on a new subject was always exciting for them all, especially if they had never followed the subject before. Criminals weren't like the police. They were normal human beings who had chosen a criminal path in life instead of following the rules created by the general public, rules that they either didn't believe in or that circumstances had forced them down. John had followed people from all walks of life and the only common denominator between them all was that they were all unpredictable. They tended not to lead regimented lifestyles where they would predictably arrive at a time and place and tended to be more ad hoc. On the whole, police officers were indoctrinated with following the rules, arriving at meetings on time and doing what they were told. Inherently there were exceptions within both worlds so they'd assess Marsden and see which he was. He was a smackhead though, so the one constant in his day would be that he would have to score some drugs. John checked his watch; they'd be there in half an hour and by then the observation post would be up and running. The intelligence staff would make sure that they could watch the main exit of the subject's building so they could let the team know. They had been briefed separately and John trusted that they would do their job well.

*** 

The intelligence officers arriving outside of the hotel at six-fifty, were dropped on the roadside by a small blue Peugeot, and with suitcases in hand, walked to the hotel main entrance. They were a male and a female, the male checking over his shoulder and looking about just before they entered. No doubt they would then go up to the upper floor room and get themselves settled for the day.

*Interesting,* thought Joe, watching it all from behind his netted curtain. *They weren't totally awful; at least they'd both arrived with suitcases, but who turns up at a hotel at seven o'clock in the morning? Nobody does in the real world; it's either after two or into the evening.*

"There we go," said Joe, as he again watched the curtain twitch in the same window as last night. So obviously the cops were after something or somebody. Joe would be a fool to think that it may not be him. They'd probably worked out that he had helped Fatty get his heroin and it was a sure bet that some grass somewhere had spoken about him. There was always some smackhead out there getting paid to tell the police what was going on and who was doing it, a person with no principles and definitely no loyalty. Was there any loyalty among the druggies? Not really. They were just interested in where their next tenner was coming from to pay for the next bag. Each dealer gang just competed with the next, vying for supremacy in this little town in the middle of nowhere. Most of the dealers were on the gear too, the real money being made by the real drugs businessmen, who controlled the supply nationally.

Joe sat back on his bed sipping from a Lucozade he'd nicked yesterday. Plans for today, none; prospects for today, none. He had his script to collect and he'd wander around the town and see what was happening. He lay back staring at the ceiling, thinking he'd give the cops an hour or so to get settled before he went out.

\*\*\*

Mary and Dave from the intelligence unit sat within a nice double bedroom in The Manderley Hotel, overlooking the address on Chandlers Terrace.

"I've sat in worse places than this," stated Dave, who was actually reclined on the double bed whilst Mary sat on a hard stool, keeping observations. "Pillows are soft and the mattress ain't too bad either," he continued.

"We are here to work," replied Mary, turning to look at him.

"You keep your eyes on that address," said Dave pointing out of the window. "We don't want to miss him." Mary looked back out of the window, laughing.

"You're a bloody goon," she said.

"Ne'er mind that. How's about I make us a nice cup of tea?" Dave stood up from the bed, putting the room kettle on. "Very nice too, a little bit of Twinings and some Scottish shortbread fingers." The brew made, Dave handed Mary a cup as her phone rang.

"Hello... oh hi Sarge. Yes, we are in and we've got a view. We can only see the front door so fingers cro... Wait! Wait! Movement at the door. The door's open. It's him!" said

Mary excitedly. "He's standing on the front doorstep, stretching; now rubbing his hands together and now stretching his legs. Looks like he's going for a run?" she continued confusedly. "Grey waterproof top, grey jogging bottoms, grey trainers. He's walking down the steps and onto the pavement. Turning left towards the town. I can't see him now." Mary's phone went dead and she looked at Dave. "They've got eyes on him," she said smiling.

"Triff," said Dave, sitting in the only armchair, "now let's see what's on telly."

***

Joe walked away from the front door of his house and turned left onto Chandlers Terrace. He thought that he had stopped long enough outside the front door to ensure that if the cops were watching him then they wouldn't miss him leaving. He didn't know if they were after him, but he thought he'd have a wander around the town and see whether he could spot any plain clothes cops. It wasn't easy to spot people following you, if they were properly trained, but he knew the town well and knew the criminals well. He just needed to bump into a few people and take it from there. Turning a corner, Joe halted and waited, looking to see if anyone followed him. After a few minutes no one appeared, apart from a scruffy old bloke with a limp, on the other side of the road, who turned left up the hill and away from Joe. Joe continued walking when he saw a couple of people he knew.

"How's things?" he asked as he approached them.

"Now then Joe, all good. You?"

"Not bad, not bad. Just to give you the heads up lads, I've heard that plain clothes might be in town today. You know, following us lot." The two males looked around suspiciously. "Keep your eyes open, boys and let anyone else you meet know too. Laters." Joe nodded and walked away from them, one of whom got immediately on his mobile phone, presumably to get the word out. Joe smiled to himself as he sauntered along. If the cops were in town, for him or not, he certainly wasn't going to make it easy for them; the more people who suspected, the better. They'd all be on the lookout and there were more addicts in the town than plain clothes cops. It would only take one of them to slip up and they'd probably sack it off for the day and go home with their tails between their legs. Joe checked the cars on the street as he walked, looking for anything out of place but spotted nothing. He knew the locations of the CCTV within the town so would avoid that initially, as it was probably manned. Turning left he took a small cut through an alley, which he knew had a low wall that he could jump over, go through two gardens and he could come out on a different street. He looked left and right and nipped into the alleyway, sprinted down, over the wall on the right, through the gardens, cut left and he appeared between two houses on a nearby street. Joe propped himself against a bin opposite the houses and stood rolling a fag and watched. The alleyway went between the houses and twisted for quite a way, so if anyone had followed him in, they'd be in there for a while. Joe heard a car engine heading at speed to the location where the alleyway would end.

*Interesting*, he thought, deciding to follow the road back to where he initially entered the alleyway. On turning a corner, his eyes were immediately drawn to a dark coloured estate vehicle with brake lights illuminated and engine running. Joe walked the pavement which would take him directly past the vehicle. Approaching, he could see that it was occupied by two males with the driver's eyes focussed on the head of the alleyway, neglecting to keep checking his rear view mirror for anyone there. Passing the vehicle, Joe glanced right, seeing a male passenger looking down at a map in his lap.

*Got you*, thought Joe, strolling past. He continued walking down the street, his initial feelings of today and last night confirmed. He was under surveillance and it could only be to do with Fatty. Turning left around the corner, he stopped to light his cigarette and sure enough heard a car door shut behind him, which would be the passenger getting out of the vehicle to follow him. He continued walking slowly down the street toward the town centre. So they'd obviously found a connection between him and Fatty and thought that they should look at him more. Try and prove something against him or find a reason to get him arrested for an offence so they could get him in custody and search his flat. Well, he'd give them a run around the town for a while, tire them and disappear for a bit. If they wanted him, they'd have to find the reason why and then come and find him. Joe had no wish to spend any time in the cells in the near future. He turned onto the precinct and wandered up to the Big Issue seller.

"Surveillance is in town, mate. Get the word around."

"Will do," replied the seller, walking forwards to offer a magazine to a likely customer.

Joe continued walking, heading towards the local Marks and Spencer. He was known by security there but hadn't been in for ages, so they would probably let him browse, following him closely. The CCTV system in there was terrific, as Joe had found out to his own detriment a few years ago, so only a fool would try to nick from there anyway. Joe entered the main door, checking the people reflected behind him in the shop mirrors as he did so. He walked through the front women's clothing area, where he knew the central escalators were and hopped on one going up, turning to face the front of the shop as he travelled. Sure enough, a man looking similar to the passenger he had seen was walking towards the escalators. Reaching the top of the escalator, Joe turned right and stepped on the descending stairs, trying not to snigger to himself. The guy following him wasn't on the ascending stairs as Joe descended, but he was happy that another member of their team would be. He clocked two women and one bloke. All looked natural but it could be any one of them and Joe was sure that it would be. Reaching the bottom, Joe headed back towards the front door of the shop and exited turning left. That was enough fun for the moment; he was thirsty and fancied a coffee and Forseti's was just around the corner. Joe strolled up to the front window and peering through, saw that Matt was sitting behind the counter, coffee in hand. He'd timed it just right and walked in.

"What is it with you?" said Matthew, looking at Joe. "You seem to have an uncanny ability to come here just when I have made myself a brew. It's like you've been watching me."

Joe laughed. "It's just luck mate. I mean if you don't want to make your poor mate a hot drink, then you don't have to." The shop entry bell sounded as a young lady walked through the door and smiled.

"Morning," said Matthew, smiling. He'd not seen her before but she was good looking and could spend as much time in his shop as she liked. Joe looked at her, then back at Matt and coughed.

"Ehhrrmm, a coffee for your mate? Or are you too busy?"

"Sorry," Matthew responded, handing him his cup. "I'll make another." The woman walked towards the back of the shop and started browsing.

"So how's things?" Matthew asked, propping open the kitchen door with his foot as he quickly made a second coffee.

"Oh, you know. Been better, been worse. On me arse,

as usual."

"Any chance of doing a proper day's work sometime?"

"Who'd employ me?" said Joe, "No one, till I get myself sorted. Mum's birthday tomorrow and I've got knack all for her." Joe looked sullenly at the floor.

"She won't mind, Joe. Just call on her, that'll be enough." Matthew's eyes still concentrated on the lady in the back. He looked at Joe.

"Better see if I can help her," he said, turning to Joe, winking and turning to move away. Matthew turned back.

"Tell you what," said Matthew, as he reached his wallet out of his pocket, removing a fiver, "get something for your mum," handing it to Joe. Matthew was no fool. He knew Joe would probably blow the cash on drugs but a fiver couldn't buy you a wrap. He walked to the rear of the store and approached the female.

"Can I help you with anything?"

That was just what Joe was waiting for. The female distracted, he headed for the door, taking off his Nike jacket in grey and reversing it to its green side. Cap on and out of the shop, he turned left, jogged to the end of the street, turning right and into an alley behind Poundsavers. He'd noticed a pushbike there yesterday whilst walking past; it was probably a staff member's, and it was there again today and insecure. *Some people were too trusting*. He jumped on it and pedalled off at speed towards the cliff gardens where he could lose anybody, hold up for a while and decide where to spend the night.

***

Two suited officers approached Sheila Wilmslow's home address, noting that her car was on the driveway and her upstairs bedroom window open, indicating that she was probably in. One of the males rang the front doorbell, could hear the chimes within the house and stepped back, awaiting a response. A woman's head popped into view, the window opened and leaning out, the female called,

"What do you want?"

"Sheila Wilmslow?" asked an officer.

"What if I am?"

"Barnston Police, Madam. We are hoping that you can assist us with our enquiries."

Sheila looked across the road to see an elderly neighbour peering out of her window inquisitively. *Well, the police had to arrive some time, best not to make any scene for the neighbours.*

"Down in two mins," she replied. The officers waited patiently on the doorstep and were shortly greeted by a robed Sheila answering the door, wearing last night's make-up and with bedraggled hair.

"Come in, come in, I'm bloody freezing," said Sheila, ushering them in. "I was just running a bath," she smiled at them both. *Handsome lads,* she thought to herself. One of the officers produced his warrant card for identification and she showed them to the living room.

"Cup of tea lads?" she asked, walking towards the kitchen, not waiting for a reply.

The officers could hear the kettle being put on, cups placed down and the chink of glass bottles. One walked towards the kitchen and popped his head around the door, to see Sheila placing a couple of empty wine bottles in a cupboard and a single glass next to the sink.

"Yes please, Sheila. Can I call you Sheila?"

"Yes of course" she replied, giving him a coy smile.

"Both milk and one sugar," replied the officer, ignoring the smile, turning back to the living room where he looked at some family photos on a side table.

"There we go," said Sheila, entering the room, hair now brushed and a big smile on her face. "Have a sit down, how can I help you?" She sat down in an armchair, tucking her bathrobe between her knees as she covered her thighs, looking directly at the second officer.

"If it's OK with you, we're going to take some notes just to help us." Sheila noted that this wasn't really a question but a statement.

"Go on," she said confusedly.

"We'll just cut to the chase. We are part of an enquiry team investigating the death of Frank Wellbury and we believe that you knew him. Please can you explain to us the nature of your relationship with Frank." *Here we go*, thought Sheila to herself. She then explained to the officers her self-employment as a cleaner and that she had been hired by Frank to clean his house. She explained that he wasn't a messy bloke, that it was a steady job that paid well and that he was a good regular customer, that she cleaned most of the house but how it was extremely rare that she would clean his office, having maybe only done so a couple of times. When asked, she didn't know if he had any bad habits and didn't really know anything much about his personal life. She cleaned once a week for him, mostly in the daytime but occasionally in the evening, when he was at home. She always travelled there in her own car and generally stayed there for a couple of hours.

"So, Sheila," the officer continued, "you can see that we are trying to get an image of what Frank was like. You haven't mentioned how you feel about his death?"

"God, it's terrible, isn't it? I couldn't believe it!" exclaimed Sheila dramatically. "Absolutely gobsmacked!"

"Right," replied officer two, watching Sheila's face

closely.

"Sorry to ask you this, Sheila," said officer one, "it's just so we have a clear understanding. Was your relationship with Frank purely professional? To clarify, did you have any personal or sexual relationship with him?"

"Moi?" she replied, raising a hand to her chest, "well his eyes wandered, you know, but he is a bloke," she laughed as her robe parted slightly at the knees. "I wouldn't be surprised if he fancied a go. I could feel him watching when I cleaned a room he was in. No, I never did, I wouldn't, I am married after all" she finished, showing the men her ring finger.

"Hubby work in town?" asked officer two.

"No, he works away in London. He's always away," she winked at him.

"Right," replied two. "That's just about us," standing up, "Oh, almost forgot! Frank's body was found last Tuesday night. When did you last see him?"

"Well, that's easy, the same night. I cleaned his house that evening."

"And where'd you go after that?"

"Straight home, I was knackered," replied Sheila.

"Husband at home when you got back?"

"No, away again," she replied with a shrug.

"That's great, Sheila, you've been really helpful and cleared up a lot of things for us. We're probably going to need to speak to you again at some point so..."

"Don't leave town!" Sheila dramatically finished the sentence for him. The officers both laughed as they walked to the front door, where Sheila let them out.

"Always here," said Sheila, winking at them again and closing the door.

The officers walked off, slightly bemused and keen to return to the office to get their reports into the system.

"She is desperate for you, mate," said officer one, laughing, punching his colleague playfully on the arm.

"Don't. What a strange woman. Clearly, hiding something, probably been shagging Frank rather than be alone at home."

"Didn't volunteer to tell us why she didn't contact the police on hearing of his death!"

"Yep, and despite the act, didn't seem surprised that he was dead." They'd reached the car, got in and travelled back to the nick to report in.

\*\*\*

Sheila closed the door and headed straight for the kitchen, where she grabbed an empty glass, tipped a short in it and necked it. Her hands were shaking as she struggled to light a cigarette, drawing deeply on it when it was lit. *That was terrible*, she felt terrible. They must have realised that she'd lied to them; they would definitely be coming back. She giggled to herself and poured another.

"Bollocks to them," she said out loud. She felt like getting pissed, downed it and poured another.

\*\*\*

Rachel sat in her own office, enjoying five minutes to herself away from the constant pressure of the enquiry. The pressure actually never eased but if she could find some solitude in the day, it felt like it did. Her mobile phone rang.

"Barnes," she announced.

"Hi Rach - it's John."

"Hi there. How's it gone?"

"To be honest... not the best. Your subject is a switched-on cookie. He's definitely on his toes about something. Straight from the off he was careful. Took a couple of strange routes to town and held still at a couple of places. Looked like anti-surveillance, but hard to tell on day one. Met up with a couple of smackheads, we got photos, and then went into town. Maybe he was expecting us, or maybe he was tipped off," John laughed. "Anyway, we lost him round about lunch." Rachel's eyes rolled to the ceiling. *Bloody lost him*, she thought.

"Only day one though Rach, we'll go back to our office and work out how we are going to cope with him tomorrow."

"OK John and I'll get the full details of what you've seen today."

"Yeah, yeah, we'll send that over." Rachel was about to put the phone down.

"Rach, Rach you still there?" asked John.

"Yeah."

"Only one other thing. He went into a bookshop in town called Forseti's. Clearly knows the guy in there, had a coffee in there with him and a chat. Seemed like friends. One of ours was in there when they were chatting."

Rachel's jaw physically dropped. Her murder subject was in Matthew's shop? *What the hell!* She felt nauseous.

"John," she said, trying to hide a tremor in her voice, "can your report on today's observations come to me and me only?"

"Yeah, no problem, speak tomorrow." The phone went dead.

Rachel placed her mobile on the desk. Her head sunk into her hands. Right, what to do with this one? She should really let the boss know but didn't really have enough detail yet. She'd get the full details emailed tomorrow and she would have a chance to see if Matthew said anything tonight when she got home. It was all probably very innocent, but one thing was for certain, she couldn't talk with Matthew about the case anymore; she'd already divulged more than she should have. It was time for home. Rachel walked out of the nick towards her car, which was parked nearby, and drove the fifteen minute drive home.

\*\*\*

"Hi love, lasagne and garlic bread for dinner if that's OK?" asked Matt, as she walked into the house. "I've just got that one out of the freezer. We made it a couple of weeks ago." He smiled, leaning towards her and giving her a peck on the cheek. "How's your day been?" he asked.

"Oh, alright," replied Rachel, "same old, same old," looking at Matt and wondering how much she really knew him. I mean, she'd known him a long time, but she was a busy person and didn't really know for sure what he got up to in his own time. He was used to her long hours but was he really happy with it? They'd never talked about long term plans, about the future, or even where they would be next year. They were drifting through life, *was this just a relationship of convenience?*

"Anyway, we always talk about me. How's your day been?" she smiled at Matt as he handed her a glass of red wine.

"Nothing much really, a few customers in, but not really sold much today."

"Oh right, none of the regulars there?"

"Not really," he replied, dishing up the food.

"What do you do all day when it's quiet?" Rachel probed.

"You know, tidy the shop, sort out the stock and invoices and then read if it is quiet. Boring stuff really, your days are so much more exciting. How's the enquiry going?"

"Slowly, slowly," replied Rachel.

"Come on Rach, you must have some juicy news. Maybe I can shed some light on things? Come up with some theories?" he laughed.

*I bet you could,* thought Rachel to herself, thinking back to the night of her initial call out. *God, being a cop made you suspicious of everything and everyone.* She recalled that Matt had been late that night. *Where had he been? Helping his little mate Joe, after Joe had murdered Wellbury?* Rachel's head was buzzing; she needed to clear it.

"More probably happens in the town centre shop consortium than in my day," said Rachel. "Shop warfare between Waterstones and Forseti's," she laughed. Matthew responded with a laugh.

"Forseti's take on the High Street chain. Where'd you even get the name?" asked Rachel.

"Oh that," Matthew laughed good naturedly, leaning forward conspiratorially, "It's a little known Norse god, the god of justice. If Waterstones knows what's good for them, they won't anger Forseti," he finished dramatically. Rachel sat back, mentally and physically exhausted.

"I'm off for a shower and an early night if that's OK Matt? I'm knackered," she smiled, stood up, gave him a peck on the cheek and headed off to the bathroom. Matthew turned, watching her leave the room. Was it something he'd said? *She must be tired*, he thought. He got up and started clearing things away, tidying the kitchen so that it was spick and span, before sitting down to watch a bit of television.

Rachel climbed into bed following her shower and could hear the TV downstairs. Matt was obviously staying up for a while. *Good*, she needed a bit of space and needed to clear her head. She picked up a book Matt had given her to read a couple of months ago; that would relax her and send her to sleep. She'd nearly finished Jodi Picoult's 'Nineteen Minutes', in essence a tale of bullying resulting in deaths and the imprisonment of a man. *Strange, what people read for relaxation.* She read on and turned the page just as officers entered a prisoner's cell. The guy was dead. Rachel sat up rereading the text. Dead in his cell, suicide, choked with his socks shoved down his throat! *That was unreal, never mind unusual; a coincidence?* Rachel read on, and after half an hour, just sat there thinking, the sounds of the television still permeating her consciousness.

# Chapter 10

Rachel arrived at work at 8 am, still tired after a restless night's sleep. Her mind was in overdrive with the ongoing surveillance, Matthew, and running the investigation in general. The surveillance team was out on the ground again today and she was expecting yesterday's resume in her inbox. She'd need to have a management meeting with Andy and Jones, to discuss yesterday's developments, but first to meet with Jim and Ben who had interviewed Wilmslow. Rachel rang Jim on his mobile phone; both were in the office so they met in a free office upstairs.

"So, gents, how did you get on with Mrs Wilmslow?" Jim took the lead, explaining how they had spoken to her at home and took Rachel through the full meeting in detail.

"If you had to summarise, just give me your general impression," asked Rachel.

"Sheila is a married woman who appears to be struggling with life at the moment. She'd either had a heavy night drinking, the night before we visited, or is a habitual drinker. She seems to be running a successful business, which would be hard if she was an alcoholic, so I'd need to question why she is drinking heavily. Hubby seems to be away a lot and with her general demeanour I'd be surprised if she hadn't had some sort of sexual relationship with our victim. She made no attempt to contact us regarding the death but admits to being at the house on the evening he was found, claiming that she went directly home afterwards. She didn't seem surprised about his death. She's a strange one, for sure. Is she hiding something? Yes. Is she a murderer? Who knows? I think she needs a formal interview at the nick, where we can challenge her account and see what happens."

"Cheers, Jim, all noted. I'll speak to the boss and we'll make some decisions. Complete your report and submit it. Good work lads." Both males stood and left the room. Rachel checked her email and saw that the surveillance report was sitting waiting for her. She read through it, printed it and went in search of Andy and Jones.

*** 

Jones, Andy and Rachel all sat in an office together and had discussed Wilmslow and the surveillance. Jones was finishing a cheese sandwich, almost spraying its contents over the officers, when Rachel disclosed that the subject had visited Forseti's bookshop.

"So, you are telling me that one of our subjects, a heroin addict no less, appears to be a close friend of your partner?" asked Jones.

"That's the impression surveillance is giving, sir," replied Rachel. This was definitely not the time to be referring to the boss by his Christian name. Rachel was nervous, she'd never been in this sort of situation before, and could kick Matthew for putting her in it.

"Have you told your partner any details about the enquiry?"

"He knows I'm on it, boss. He knows that it's a murder enquiry," she replied. Jones looked at Rachel, clearly thinking what he should do and reached his decision.

"Right, I've not run any enquiry where some crap like this doesn't rear its head. It's either rumours of personal relationships or corrupt police officers that usually put a spanner in the works. You are a good officer, Rachel, and I don't want to lose you off this investigation, thanks for coming to me straight away. It will change my approach on the enquiry but that's not necessarily a bad thing.

Your partner – Matthew, is it? - will need to be spoken to as a witness at some point. You need to let Complaints and Discipline know of your relationship with Matthew and of his with a criminal. How's the surveillance going?" asked Jones, looking at Andy. That was it. The boss hadn't exploded and Rachel was still on the enquiry. She breathed a quiet sigh of relief, lesson learnt.

"Obs have been on for five hours now boss, with no sightings of the subject," he grimaced. "If you want my opinion, then I think he spotted the team yesterday and is on his toes. He definitely has something to hide."

"Bloody surveillance!" exclaimed Jones. "Couldn't even manage to follow my granny if they tried. Well, we are where we are. Rachel, I want a search team organised. Andy, I want a warrant authorised by the magistrates to search Marsden's flat. Let's shake the tree a bit and see what falls."

***

Mrs Briggs finished packing the kids' cases and carried them downstairs from their bedrooms to the hallway, where her own was waiting. Sebastian was at work, he was due to have a busy week, and would join them later on. Half term was due and she was taking the kids out of school two days prior, so that they could have a long weekend with grandparents at Center Parcs, Whinfell. The kids loved it there and having grandparents along meant that Mrs Briggs could get some relaxation time to herself and enjoy some well-deserved spa treatments. Sebastian would join them at their luxury lodge by Saturday. Opening the front door, she traipsed to and fro, placing her cases in the rear of her Volvo XC90 and after a final trip, returned to shut the front door. House secure, and it was time to go. A quick text sent to Sebastian, she started the engine and departed the driveway.

Mrs Briggs didn't realise that she had been watched from a small copse of trees set on a rise to the left of the house. Patience had paid out, as it usually did to those who waited, and provided the onlooker their first glimmer of hope for an opportunity. Cases packed, adult's and the kid's, meant that she would be gone for a few days. *A few days away with the family, how lovely,* they thought, *I wonder what Sebastian will get up to in your absence?* The figure walked through the copse, away from the house to an adjacent street, collecting their pushbike before exiting, and headed further to the south side to watch Briggs' walk home.

***

Jane's task force team had been briefed for the execution of the warrant. Each member of the team was given specific tasks to ensure that it was a thorough and organised search. The team were all search trained and had searched numerous rooms, houses and buildings in the past, so were well versed in the role. Jane was in charge of controlling the search and two of the staff were already in protective equipment to force entry to the building and flat if necessary. The team were deployed in a van near to the premises; two detectives would approach the front door to see if it was open as the team approached. Jane had also deployed two of her staff in plain clothes near the rear of the property; they were to cover any rear exits once the team approached. Searches for the team were ten a penny but today Rachel could feel the tension in the van. They had to get this one right, with two doors and a couple of flights of stairs to negotiate before getting in the flat, it wouldn't be easy. Rachel pressed transmit on her radio and spoke calmly.

"OK everyone, move forward." The van started moving slowly, turning a corner, which afforded Rachel a full view down the street towards the house door.

"Rear exits secure," transmitted over the radio by her officers, as she watched the plain clothes detectives approach the front door, trying the door handle. The van speed increased. A detective turned, giving an 'OK' signal with his hand.

"Steadily in," said Rachel to the driver. The rear crew cracked the side door, ready for a quick exit.

"Approaching the address," Jane transmitted. Adrenaline pumped "Strike, strike, strike," transmitted louder.

The van pulled outside the address. The side door opened. Two officers exited first, with shield and red door enforcer. Two more came out behind, Jane last. They ran up the steps and through the open door. Detectives followed. Quickly and quietly up the stairs. Flat identified. Handles tried. Secure.

"Police, stand back!" shouted Jane at the top of her voice. Then 'BANG!' the door knocked out of its frame by Hogan.

"In, in, in," by the team who entered the flat.

"Empty!" shouted an officer, to Jane in the corridor.

"Flat secure," transmitted Jane. The detectives had been briefed to find the rear door of the building on entry, which they had done with no signs of the subject having scarpered. Jane rang Rachel.

"Hi Rach, we're in. No issues but no sign of your boy. We'll get the search started. I'll let you know if we find anything," and the call terminated. The team all together now, prepared to search the flat. The same process was used on every search to ensure that no mistakes were made. Rachel would monitor everyone, supervising the search, an officer was designated to take all exhibits seized and to complete relevant paperwork, an officer would stand at the flat door so that no persons entered and the remaining officers would be split into two pairs. The two pairs would conduct the search, with one searching and the other observing that person searching. The couples would alternate their search and watch and they would divide the room up between them as necessary. This would be a thorough search and would take some time. The detectives were just present as extra bodies but Rachel didn't want them searching. Detectives were notoriously poor at searching correctly. They may have skills in other areas but searching was definitely not one of them. On a quick scan of the room, Rachel had noticed straight away the Rockport coat, which was lying over the bed and she pointed it out to one of the search pairs.

"Yep, we're having that, Sarge," he replied, acknowledging to Rachel that he understood its significance.

The flat was a bit of a tip, typical of an addict's flat and the officers needed to be careful. Some users left used needles discarded indiscriminately, which could cause them a needle stick injury; cleanliness was not always at the forefront of an addict's mind. The kitchen cupboard had a sharps box hidden within it and next to it, a small bag of crystalline powder which was probably citric acid. Burnt foil lay in various places in the flat and a couple of tablespoons with burnt marks thereon; all the marks of a drug abuser who was inhaling and injecting heroin. It would take a while to do the complete search. Jane rang Rachel to inform her about the coat.

***

Walking into the intelligence cell, Rachel saw Andy.

"They've found a Rockport coat matching our description at Marsden's."

"Great," Andy replied.

"I've told the boss. We're going to circulate him as wanted on suspicion of murder. We've got the intelligence about drug supply, we have the coat, he's a similar build to the guy on the CCTV and the unknown male is the only person we know of that has accessed the house within the time frame that we believe he was murdered. He's been raised to suspect status; the boss is ringing the Chief. Can we get briefing items completed for the shift briefings? I'll speak to the control room and brief some officers to start the search for him."

***

Joe sat in the front room at his mother's house, having slept there the night before. He'd received a call late yesterday from a friend, telling him that the police were searching his flat and that he'd better look out for himself. His suspicions about being followed had been correct then and could only relate to Frank. His mum walked into the lounge with a cup of tea.

"There you go dear. Would you like some toast?"

He took a sip of the sweet tea.

"Ooh! What's that car outside?" his mum continued, moving to the front window and peering through the netted curtains. "It looks like a police car." There was a solid knock at the front door. Joe choked on his mouthful and sprang up, his cup falling to the floor. His mum screamed. He shot out of the lounge door to the hallway and saw the shape of two persons at the door.

"Shit," said Joe, balancing to get his trainers on. Nearly stumbling, he careened towards the back door.

126

Reaching for the handle slowly he chinked the door. Wham! The door flew open, catching his head and knocking him backwards, as he saw a dark shoulder moving forward. His head swam as a hand grabbed him, pulling him forwards and down to the carpet, the weight of a body landed on him.

"Police! You're under arrest!" shouted a male voice. The weight shifted as Joe's arm was taken and a wrist lock placed on it, effectively pinning him to the ground. Still dazed, he was in no condition to resist as his other arm was pinned and a set of handcuffs placed on. Police officers sat him up.

"You are going nowhere, son," said a grizzly-faced cop. "Joe Marsden, you are under arrest on suspicion of murder. You do not have to say anything. But, it may harm your defence if you do not mention when questioned something which you later rely on in court. Anything you do say may be given in evidence." Joe sat there silently; the bottom had just dropped out of his world. His mum stood in the kitchen, dumbstruck, hands held up to a face twisted in anguish.

"What have you done, Joe?"

Joe sat silent, chin dropping to his chest.

"Let's get him out of here," said Grizzly, as they stood Joe up and led him out of the door. Two more cops entered the kitchen and Joe walked to the car, hearing only the woeful sobs coming from his mum.

***

Barnston Police Custody was situated on the ground floor of the building and could be accessed via an external garage with a roller shutter door. The police car sat within the parking bay as the roller shutter door closed and that was it; Joe's liberty was truly taken away. He was led through the solid metal custody door into the building and placed into a holding cage. Grizzly looked at Joe.

"Right mate, I'm gonna remove your handcuffs for you and I don't want you kicking off or they'll go straight back on. You're here now and you know that there is no way out unless we let you out. So be a good lad and behave." Joe silently held up his handcuffed wrists, indicating that he wanted the cuffs off. Grizzly, supported by his colleague, gently removed the cuffs. Joe had been thoroughly searched in the van, so had no items on him which could cause harm to himself or another. He rubbed his wrists, which were chafed, and felt his head, where a nice egg had formed due to the collision with the kitchen door. Grizzly walked off to see the custody sergeant, Joe remained silent.

"Custody Sergeant's ready for you mate," said Grizzly, returning to the holding cage and removing him from the barred area. They walked to the desk, behind which stood a middle aged, tubby police officer, with specs parked on his head.

"Step forward." Joe did so. "Now, I know you've been through the system before but just so you are clear, my job here is to look after you, to make sure that you are treated fairly and to ensure that everyone's actions are within the law. First things first, I'm going to take your details." The sergeant moved behind a computer, placing his specs on and looking over the top, stated, "Officer."

"Sarge," replied Grizzly. "This male has been arrested on suspicion of the murder of a Mr Frank Wellbury. I believe that CID will be down shortly with full circumstances. The Sergeant looked at Grizzly, harrumphed and started the booking in procedure. Joe answered the required questions but when asked about the injury on his head, stated, "I was assaulted when I was arrested." The sergeant noted his comment on the custody record and also noted Joe's head injury.

"Do you require a solicitor?" asked the sergeant.

"Sebastian Briggs," Joe replied.

"OK, I'll contact him. Right, that's you booked in. Two more things; one, I am authorising seizure of all your clothing and your footwear. We will provide you with replacements whilst in custody. Two, I will contact the duty doctor who you will see. I note that you are a heroin addict. He or she will assess your needs and also check that head of yours. Constable, if you can do the necessary and put him in cell twelve when you're done?" Grizzly led Joe away to the cell, where his colleague was waiting to assist in the seizure of his clothing. Now, as well as being banged up, he would have to strip in front of these two goons. Joe stood on a large square of paper which had been placed on the floor and under the direction of the officers, methodically stripped off his clothes, as they seized and exhibited them. Finally, the officers folded the large square of paper which they exhibited too, its purpose to have captured any fibres that had fallen off their prisoner whilst changing. He was given a navy blue sweat top and pants and a pair of black plimsolls in return.

"Right mate, that's us done," said Grizzly, exiting the cell, "and this is your home for the foreseeable future. You're in an observation cell." Grizzly pointed to a small CCTV camera high up in the cell corner and turned to look at Joe who sat disconsolately on his bed. The officer shut the door with a metallic thud.

\*\*\*

Sheila had just got off the phone from Sebastian.

Lovely, his wife had gone away for a few days so they'd be able to meet up at his beautiful house and have a romantic night in. He'd no doubt have some takeaway delivered for them and he'd supply some lovely wine. Sheila loved climbing into that lovely big Jacuzzi bath of his, the one which she usually had to clean, and lying back in luxury as they chatted. She'd also be able to stay over and enjoy time in his bed with him. Why couldn't she have married a man like Seb? Someone who cared, like him. Someone who would look after her properly. Well, at least she had the opportunity to get spoiled by somebody, some of the time. Sheila walked out to her car, where she climbed in and set off to do a day's work.

***

Matthew sat in the bay window of Costa, looking across the road. He'd decided not to open up the shop today, as he had other things that he needed to get on with. The town of Barnston was slowly stirring to life; the shops all open and a few pedestrians strolling around the precinct. Trade would pick up but it was generally quiet at this time of year. Matthew sat with a book in hand, about to start reading, when he saw Sebastian Briggs exiting his business premises in a hurry and on the phone. Briggs stood outside, looking up and down, then terminated his call and fastened his coat. *He was always a strange, smarmy guy*, thought

Matthew, *I wonder where he's going?* Standing up, Matthew grabbed his coffee and headed out of the door. Briggs had turned left and was walking towards the top of town. Matthew followed on the opposite side at a safe distance. Head down, with a purposeful stride, Briggs clearly was on a mission. He turned right in the general direction of the police station, as Matthew crossed the road to ensure he had a wide angled view of Briggs. Just as he was preparing to cross, Briggs jumped as a little red Corsa pipped at him, bringing him out of his single minded reverie. Matthew watched as a pretty looking lady driving the car waved at Briggs, he responded with a big smile and wave. The car continued along the road, passing Matthew, who read the advertisement 'Sheila's Maid' signposted on the side of the car. *Interesting association*, Matthew noted, *work or social friend?* The car drove off and Briggs continued walking in the general direction of the police station, where he entered the front door. Another client for Briggs to look after and more money put in his pocket. Matthew returned to Costa following his little sojourn. Barnston was a small town where everyone seemed to know everyone and a town where it was hard to get away with anything without being seen. Matthew wondered how Rachel's case was going as he sat back down once again to finish his book. Niederman's book wasn't bad and was a stark warning to any practising law firm. *Maybe Briggs should read it?* thought Matthew, *it may enlighten him on a few things.*

He stayed in Costa for another half hour and finished the book. He'd have to find something else now, maybe another genre. As a bookseller he tried to read as much variety as he could to be able to offer recommendations and discuss opinions with his customers. He'd already looked in Waterstones' window this morning and thought he'd just nip to the library. It was good to keep in touch with them and show his face once in a while. Good for business relations and who knows they may point some people in his shop's direction, in an effort to support local trade. The library was nice and airy, he said hello to a couple of purple clad staff members as he entered. He'd have a quick browse to show willing, though any books he wanted, he would just get from the shop. What was that book Rach was reading last night? She'd marked a page towards the back of it; The Jodi Picoult, if he remembered rightly, 'Nineteen Minutes'. He searched the shelves, locating the book and scanned the back cover. Very apt at the moment, considering her current murder case; people killed, bullying at the forefront and yes, there's the page, he said quietly to himself, having scanned a load of pages. A man found dead with socks shoved down his throat. *Was it a coincidence or a clue?* Matthew loved this cloak and dagger world that Rachel was part of. He'd have to try and wheedle his way in again and see how her investigation was going. After all, it's not every day you get to be part of a murder mystery.

# Chapter 11

Sebastian introduced himself at the front counter to a young female receptionist who rang the custody suite to let them know that he was there and asked a staff member to collect him.

"I can go through myself if you want, I know the way," he joked in his oily fashion. The staff member just looked him up and down and dismissively responded, "Sit down sir, someone will fetch you shortly," turning away and walking into the back office. Briggs wasn't well liked in the police station and he knew it, although he still felt that he should be shown a modicum of respect and not made to sit in the public waiting area. After about five minutes waiting, he stood up, preparing to ring the bell, about to extol the unfairness of his client having to wait for legal advice, when the interior door opened and a male voice spoke, "Mr Briggs, this way."

Briggs walked through the door and was met by a middle aged, uniformed jailor, who marched him into the custody suite. Clearly ex- military, with his practiced gait and impeccable uniform.

"Morning Sergeant," greeted Briggs with a large grin.

"Mr Briggs," replied the sergeant, turning to the jailor, "Please can you get Mr Marsden from his cell and take him to Interview Room One," handing him a large bunch of keys. The jailor walked off rattling and returned with Joe.

"Joe," stated Briggs, by way of greeting.

"Sebastian," replied Joe.

Briggs turned towards the custody sergeant.

"Well, I'll take my client into Interview Room One, Sergeant. Please can I have any disclosure documents that have been prepared?" he asked. "I'd imagine that we will be together for a while, so a cup of coffee for each of us would be lovely, thanks," with a smile remaining on his face. *Arrogant tosser*, thought the sergeant, but responded, "Of course, that won't be a problem and the jailor will take you to the room," he smiled in response. The jailor walked Briggs and Joe to the interview room, where they would be left alone to allow Joe his private consultation. The custody sergeant rang the enquiry team, informing them that Briggs was here and was requesting disclosure. The team had already prepared a disclosure document, which would detail anything that would assist the defence in preparing their client's defence, disclosing the material reasons why their client had been arrested. The olden days of holding evidence back to 'surprise' criminals during an interview had gone. Now the police had to lay their cards on the table so that they were being totally fair to the detainee.

Shortly afterwards, the jailor knocked on the door of Interview Room One, waited five seconds and entered, carrying two coffees. A detective stood at the custody desk and when asked, Briggs stepped out and was handed an A4 sheet of paper containing the disclosure statement.

"Thank you, Detective," stated Briggs, taking the paper and returning to the room where Joe sat head in hands. The door closed behind Briggs as he re-entered his confidential briefing.

***

Joe looked at Briggs, who was examining the document he had been handed.

"What have they got?" asked Joe, looking at Briggs expectantly.

"Nothing too much to worry about," replied Briggs, glancing at Joe, continuing to read as he sat down on his chair and sipped his coffee. He placed the sheet of paper down on the table and reached for his pen and notebook. They'd both already had a discussion and Briggs had noted Joe's injuries, thinking that a case of police brutality may help to muddy the waters.

"Right Joe, the first thing that we are going to do is a no reply interview. By that I mean that when you are asked any question then you are going to sit there quietly and say nothing."

"What's on the bloody sheet of paper, Sebastian?" repeated Joe, his face flushing and voice rising in anger.

"Oh, nothing really. Date of Wellbury's death. CCTV of the possible offender, who they believe matches your description, attending the address on the night of the offence. A Rockport coat seized from your flat which they believe the offender was wearing on the night they committed the offence. No forensics back yet, but they expect them to prove your involvement."

"Bloody hell," said Joe. "They're really going to town on me."

"Right, back to what we will do at the interview. Now, it's hard to ..."

Joe interrupted, "You've not even asked me if I did it?" said Joe, voice still raised.

In the custody suite, the jailor could hear the raised voice in the room and reported it to the sergeant. It was a police station, so the sergeant wasn't overly worried. If the client and their solicitor wanted to fall out then that was up to them, as long as it didn't result in fisticuffs. They'd monitor the situation and check on them in twenty minutes.

"Well, I don't really care," replied Briggs. "You either did it or you didn't, but surely you want me to get you out of this police station as soon as I can? Unless you wish to confess to everything of course, which means I get out of here quicker, you stay in and I still get my fees, but for a lot less work."

"You're such a git," replied Joe, more sullenly.

"I may well be but I'm the one who is going to get you out of here, if you let me."

The tenseness in the room dissipated as Briggs continued to consult with his client, confident that Marsden would taste fresh air by teatime. The trick for many of these matters was not in whether the client was being honest but in whether they would follow the solicitor's instructions. If the police had enough to charge the client at this time, then they would state that. If not, they were reliant on the client saying something in an interview. If the client said nothing then they had nothing to work with. Briggs set about drafting a prepared statement which essentially would state that Joe was not guilty, had not attended the address and knew nothing surrounding the circumstances of the death. Briggs would present this to the interviewing detectives prior to the interview and advise them that the client would say nothing more. This was the farce played out at many custodial interviews and Briggs was an expert at it.

*** 

Twenty minutes later Briggs opened the interview door, popped his head round it, seeing the jailor.

"Ready when you are," he smiled at the jailor. "If you could let the desk sergeant know that my client could do with the loo and then something to eat, that would be great."

The jailor entered the room and collected Joe, returning him to his cell to urinate whilst he waited outside. Returning to the interview room, waiting on the table was a McDonald's meal.

"Fine cuisine at its best," joked Briggs.

Shortly after, a further knock on the door and two detectives entered. Briggs stood up and offered a handshake in greeting which was ignored by both the officers. Joe finished his meal and a detective placed the rubbish in a bin in the corner.

The interview started as Joe was given all of his legal warnings and the audio recording machine spun round whilst the detectives talked. True to his advice, the only words that left Joe's mouth were "No reply." Joe gave this reply to every question asked of him from, "What is your name," to "Does this Rockport coat belong to you?" Advice was given by the police to him regarding his silence and what this may mean. The officers gave Joe every opportunity to give his side of the story. Joe ignored it all, hard though it was at first, the monotony of the questioning driving into him. He was sweating and shaky, despite the prescribed diazepam he had been given, he desperately needed a fix. Joe just wanted all of this to go away so that he could get out and score. His addiction was paramount in his throbbing head and he just wished everyone would shut up.

"That's the conclusion of this interview," stated one of the detectives.

"I'd like to make my representation to the desk sergeant regarding bail please," stated Briggs.

"Just give us five minutes, Mr Briggs. If you stay here with Joe we'll go and see him." The detectives exited the room.

"Well done, Joe. You did really well there," said Briggs.

Joe just sat there silently, shaking and sweating. He just wanted to get out, he needed to get out.

"Are they gonna give me bail?" he asked.

"Oh yes, they're going to have to. They have nothing to link you forensically yet. All they have is your coat and an image of someone, who cannot be identified, attending Wellbury's house. They've got nothing solid and you have told them nothing. To be honest, I think your arrest was a desperate attempt to get a confession."

Briggs peeked around the door to see what appeared to be a drunken tramp leaning against the custody desk. He seemed barely able to talk and he stank of sweat and urine. He could smell him from here. Briggs quickly closed the door, almost gagging.

"It's safer here, Joe. There's some sort of creature getting booked in." Briggs wiped his hands with a neatly pressed handkerchief, produced from his pocket, as if cleansing them after touching the door. "Hope it's not catching," he laughed. Joe just looked at him.

"So, I'm going to speak with the custody sergeant and sort your bail. I can complete all the necessary paperwork for your fees later. Once you're getting bailed, I'll be out the front and we can have a little chat about anything I may need."

Joe just looked at him. He was in here, for the most serious offence any person could be, and *Briggs was only interested in lining his own pockets and looking at what was in it for himself. Self-centred and rich, just like Fatty was. Well, everyone knew what had happened to Fatty.*

Briggs checked out the door again and seeing the jailor, called him over. The custody desk was free and the air now being sprayed liberally with Oust odour eliminator.

"Just watch him, or put him back in his cell," stated Briggs, walking towards the desk. He walked away, giving the jailor no option but to attend to the prisoner.

"Now Sergeant," stated Briggs, approaching the desk.

"Mr Briggs. No need to start your representations. The investigators have been in contact and will not be opposing bail. I'll be releasing your client just as soon as

I have completed the paperwork. John, bring him here," finished the sergeant, talking to the jailor. Briggs turned to Joe.

"OK Joe, that's you sorted. I'll see you out the front in about ten. If I can just leave with this officer, Sergeant?" Briggs indicated to a police constable just leaving, who waited.

"Yes Mr Briggs," replied the Sergeant, turning to Joe and dismissing Briggs.

Sebastian followed the police constable and was shown out of the front of the building. On exiting he took a deep breath of fresh air before reaching into his inside pocket and pulling out a Montecristo cigar, lighting it, enjoying the taste and aroma.

Joe stood at the custody desk, waiting to be booked out.

"We'll be keeping all your clothes that we seized and also your mobile phone. If eventually they are not needed in the investigation, they'll be returned to you. You've got no cash but no doubt your mate Mr Briggs will lend you some."

"He's no mate of mine, I bloody hate him," replied Joe.

"Well, he's managed to help you get bail today, son."

"Yeah, but at what price?" replied Joe.

The desk sergeant looked at the jailor after handing Joe his bail sheet.

"Right John, can you show him out please?"

With that, Joe was escorted from the station and shown out of the front door of the police station, where Briggs was waiting for him.

Joe walked out into the fresh air and took a deep breath, giving a sigh of relief. Briggs stood there in a plume of smoke and smiled.

"So, Joe, bailed to your mum's address. Not a bad

result."

"Yes, thank you Sebastian," he replied.

"Now Joe, about our little matter of payment. Obviously, as I said, I'll sort all the legal fees. You got any money on you?"

"Not a scratch."

Briggs started walking away from the police station and turned a corner into a side street, followed by Joe. He reached into his back pocket and pulled out a fat brown leather wallet and pulled three tenners from it.

"What I'd like from you Joe, is to see you tomorrow. Probably best up by the cliff monument at six in the evening. I'll need a little bit of a pick me up for the evening. You know a little bit of coke. There's twenty pounds there to help you buy. I know it'll be more but you're a resourceful chap. I'll pay the rest, and a tip, when we meet." Joe just looked at him distastefully. "Come on Joe, you know the score, we've been here before." He handed the cash to Joe in a closed handshake. "Oh, I've also popped a tenner extra in there for you, I'm sure that you'll be needing to score." With that, he smiled and walked away.

Joe walked away, cash in hand. *What an arrogant bloke Briggs was.* He couldn't escape the fact that he'd got him out of custody but *he was a two faced bent solicitor. He was known for it through the town but got away with it countless times. Who was ever going to have a go at Briggs and his criminal lifestyle? Why didn't the police ever investigate and arrest him? He was a 'Fat cat' just like Wellbury was, sponging off the disadvantaged people in life. It was time Briggs got his comeuppance.* Joe could always tell the police. Nah, they wouldn't believe him and they'd do nothing about it anyway. He may just take the thirty pounds and stuff Briggs' request. That would be a small summary justice, though Briggs deserved so much more.

***

Richard sat alone in his flat as he did now, every single night of his life. He hadn't always been alone but now life seemed to have taken him down that path. In his early twenties Richard had a close relationship with a woman called Anna. She had lived on the outskirts of town and he had first met her on the train to Fenchurch. She was such a bubbly character, a total contrast to Richard, which seemed to make it all work. That first journey they had chatted together, Richard at first shyly, but when he saw her laughing with him, his confidence grew. Arriving in Fenchurch, they even went for a coffee together before parting company with an exchange of telephone numbers. Over the next few months, they met frequently in Barnston, going for coffees, walks by the sea, and a couple of pub meals. Richard was falling in love. Anna lived with her parents and Richard had his own flat. He'd started his 'medical career' at the hospital, which he'd told Anna about; she initially, was not working. Then she landed a job at Wellbury's store as part of the retail team. Although not a terrific paying job, she was over the moon. Richard never divulged his past history with the owner, as Anna seemed happy and that was fine with him. He recalled it being a Friday when he met with Anna and his world began to change. They met in town for a coffee, when out of the blue, Anna asked him "What is it that you actually do at the hospital, Rich? I've never really asked you."

Richard felt slightly nauseous; he'd never really told her. Sure, he may have embellished things a little bit, made himself sound more important than he was but all guys do that.

"Well, you know. Look after the patients, assess their needs, help with their treatments," he replied. Anna frowned at him, "Frank says that you're a hospital porter," she stated.

"Oh, it's Frank, is it?" replied Richard, his stomach knotting.

"Yeah, he says you just wheel people around all day. I didn't know that. I thought you were a doctor or something."

"Well, well I never said that, Anna," he said, hesitantly. "You know, I help people," he stuttered.

"Mmmm," she looked at him as if assessing him. "I don't know if you've been totally honest," she stated casually. Richard sat hands under the table, fists clenched, feeling anger stirring, hatred simmering. *Bloody Wellbury on his case again.*

"Frank seems like a good man," mused Anna, oblivious to Richard's mounting reaction. "Right, that's me," she said, standing up, "got to get back to work. Frank wants me to look at redesigning his office with him." Anna pecked Richard on the cheek, said, "See you later," turned and walked out.

Richard sat there looking at the empty chair in front of him and that was the day that his life changed.

***

During the next couple of months, Anna started retreating from his life. She never seemed able to meet with him, frequently didn't respond to texts; the relationship had changed dramatically. Richard realised that he could have been honest from the beginning but it was only a small lie of omission, nothing that deserved this type of treatment by her. He couldn't believe that once again Wellbury was affecting his life so much. He hated him. Richard tried writing to Anna, called at her parents, sat near her house in the hope of seeing her. He didn't want to and he'd been holding back but he'd have to try and catch her leaving the shop. That was the day he saw them, Wellbury leaving the shop just before closing time, arm in arm with Anna. Anna had been looking up at him and laughing at something he'd said. They were clearly a couple, happy together. He knew Wellbury's reputation, his poor treatment of women hadn't changed through the years and Anna had fallen for it. *What a stupid cow!* What a stupid idiot Wellbury was for stealing his woman, ruining his life.

Richard turned and walked away. Nothing ever went right for him; he was destined to be alone forever. Over the next few days, he was a mess; not washing, not eating. He'd rung in sick at work. Mentally he flipped between sobbing, rage and numbness. If only he could speak with Anna, warn her, let her know what Wellbury was like, she might understand. That's when he found himself, a pale, unshaved man resembling a down and out, near her address, at the small outer railway station where she had first got on the train. He looked to the platform where eight people were standing in their drab raincoats, waiting for the train. Except for one lady who stood in a bright red mac with a matching umbrella. He couldn't believe it and smiled; it was Anna. Now was his chance. He walked to the platform.

"Anna."

Anna stood on the platform waiting for her train to Fenchurch. The train to Barnston would come shooting past in a minute, returning in about ten minutes to collect the passengers for Fenchurch. People milled about near her in their drab coats, shoulders shrugged high, protecting exposed necks from the elements. The tracks rumbled, indicating a train coming.

"Anna," she heard her name and turned.

Before her stood a tramp, a male, unkempt, unwell and clearly in need of help. His clothing looked filthy, his bearded face and dishevelled greasy hair poking out from under his hood. Who the hell was this? He walked towards her with a leer or was it a smile on his face. Anna involuntarily stepped back. The train tracks rattled. Her eyes focussed on the male. He moved forward. She retreated again. People nearby, oblivious.

"Anna, it's me," said the male grinning, his voice almost drowned by the approaching train.

She looked. He moved forward quickly, hand reaching out. She jumped back.

"SCCRREEEEEEECH!" train brakes squealed. A woman screamed. The man's hand withdrew.

Richard watched Anna fall straight in front of the approaching train. Chaos ensued. Screeching train, screaming woman. "Oh God!" from a male on the platform. Richard in shock.

"No, no, no!" he'd only wanted to talk. He turned and walked away from the platform. At a safe distance he picked up his speed and ran, heading for his flat, panicking. He'd not just lost Anna; he would never see her again. He got to his flat door and entered where he curled on his bed, sobbing.

Richard would never forget that day. It was rare that he allowed himself to think of it. The police had never found 'the tramp' who may have been a witness to Anna's tragic death. The parents would never find out why the daughter they love chose to kill herself in such a way. Wellbury would never have the woman he stole from Richard and now ironically, Wellbury would never again ruin anybody else's life.

***

144

Rachel walked out of the office after debriefing the investigators following their interview with her suspect. The interview had gone as expected and no terrific gains had been made. At least they now had the Rockport coat and the suspect's phone and clothing. Interrogation of the phone may provide the evidence needed or forensics may come up with something on the clothing or the coat. The team had gone as far as they could with Marsden for the moment, so it would be back to the grindstone to try to prove his involvement. Meanwhile, there was still work to do around the cleaner and continuation of all the house to house enquiries. The CCTV team had evidenced 'Rockport' leaving the house about twenty minutes after attending but again there were no facial images of this person. A trawl of the CCTV in the area may reveal more. The source unit had been tasked to get someone close to Marsden. Whatever they turned up, Marsden would be coming back in for a more detailed interview in the future.

Rachel was due to meet Matt in town so that they could go out for something to eat together. She didn't really feel up to it but as she approached the railway station, she saw Matthew standing beaming, holding a single red rose. She laughed. Cheesy as it was, she always seemed to fall for his charm. Walking up, she gave him a quick hug and a peck on the cheek.

"I've booked us into the fish restaurant in ten minutes," said Matt. "Fresh fish caught today with a good selection. A couple of glasses of wine and a taxi home? I'll drive you in tomorrow."

"Sounds great," said Rachel, taking his arm as they wandered to the restaurant. They sat down at a table for two and sipped on their chilled white wines, both aware that recently they had spent little time together. Moments like these should be cherished and both were trying to do so.

"Well, I'm sure that you've had a busy day as usual, Rach, but quite honestly, I've sat around doing very little all day."

"OK for some," replied Rachel, smiling.

"You should try it. You work too hard. We need to start thinking about going away on holiday sometime soon. Get a well-earned rest. Maybe after this murder investigation, what do you think?"

"God, I would love that, Matt. I don't know when I'll finish on it, but hopefully we'll make some breakthrough."

"Fingers crossed," replied Matt, with fingers literally crossed. "You were fast asleep when I got to bed last night."

"Yeah, I read for a bit then dozed off," she replied.

"I moved your book. You finished it? Horrible suicide," he exclaimed.

Rachel looked at him. "The socks," she stated.

"That's the one." Neither person missed the significance of the method. Matthew didn't want to push anything.

"Well, I sat and read in Costa for an hour this morning. 'The Devil's Advocate', do you remember seeing the film? Al Pacino and Keanu Reeves about a law firm in New York. Little bit grizzly."

"I remember it," replied Rachel, beginning to relax. Rachel and Matthew kept the conversation light. It seemed ages since they had actually last spent some quality time together and tonight was what they both needed.

# Chapter 12

## January 2016

Frank departed the shop, leaving his staff with a wave of his hand and a "Good work," hollered to them. He was feeling tired and at three o'clock in the afternoon had done enough work for today. His car was parked behind the store in his own private parking space but he decided to leave it there for a while whilst he nipped to a nearby pub. He loved an afternoon pint or two if he could fit it into his busy schedule before heading home for some stronger stuff. Sheila would be round to clean later on so he could sit back and enjoy her company and watch her backside jiggling as she dusted. He'd tried it on a couple of times with her, making her laugh, but she'd never given him the go ahead. He didn't really want to upset her as he couldn't be bothered finding another cleaner. She did a good job for him and was good looking to boot, so he had no real complaints.

He walked into the bar where Brian, the landlord, greeted him and immediately started pulling a pint of Guinness.

"How's business?" asked Brian.

"Same old same old, mate," replied Frank, "not complaining. Keeping me fed and watered," he took the pint from Brian, took a swig and ordered a whisky chaser too. "Stick it on my tab."

Frank looked around the pub, which was fairly quiet. A couple sat in a corner booth finishing their wines, empty plates indicating that they'd had some lunch, an old boy wearing specs sat by the fire reading a book whilst enjoying a drink and the warmth, whilst at the bandit a bloke stood with his back to Frank popping coins in and losing. The television was on behind the bar, displaying some images of Tim Peake's first space walk with subtitles extolling his achievement.

"Bloody idiot," Frank mumbled to himself.

"What was that?" said the old guy who had stepped from the fire to the bar.

"Oh, nothing. He must be mad, that's all," replied Frank gesturing to Peake.

"A brave man though, a brave man," reflected the old boy. "A pint of Landlord sir please," he asked the landlord.

"I'm just going to change the barrel. Give me two." Brian went round the back of the bar and disappeared, presumably to the cellar. The old man turned to look at the mesmerising flames and Frank finished his pint.

"Watch that for me will you," Frank stated heading to the toilet.

"Indeed I will," replied the old man, continuing to watch the fire.

Frank headed to the toilet and the man on the bandit finished his last spin and turned to the bar.

"Oh well, can't win every day" he said in a local accent, placing his glass next to Frank's empty one at the bar. Taking some coins out of his pocket he dropped one on the floor. The old man bent to pick it up.

"There you go," he said, handing it back. The youngster placed six pounds on the counter, payment for his pint before saying "Cheers," and leaving the pub. The room now empty, the old boy pushed the empties away looking at Frank's whisky. He picked up the glass and gave the whisky a gentle rotation, smelling the peatiness of the amber liquid. He loved that smell that reminded him of good times and younger days, he then placed the glass back down, wandering back to the fire.

The landlord returned to the bar, pulled through the beer and once happy, served a pint of Landlord. The coins and glasses were collected and Frank returned to the bar, picking up the whisky. He also smelt the whisky before upending the glass and throwing the contents down his throat. Happy with a pleasant end to his day, he said goodbye to Brian and left the bar to the bright lights outside. Although he didn't particularly care for law and order, Frank didn't particularly want to lose his licence so decided he'd better drive home now, before the drink really hit his system. That whisky wasn't the best, leaving a bitter taste in his mouth; he'd have to whinge at Brian next time and no doubt would get a free short from him.

Frank walked to his car ignoring all passers-by and fumbling with his key fob, squinted to identify the remote unlock button thinking he'd really have to get his eyes tested soon. The car unlocked successfully and Frank climbed into the driver's seat, started the engine and unconcernedly placed the public of Barnston at risk as he drove home. Frank arrived home ten minutes later where his gated drive opened and welcomed him into his demesne.

\*\*\*

Climbing out of the car, Frank felt sweaty and slightly nauseous, the bitterness still in his mouth but fading. He needed just a little bit of 'brown' to chill him. He'd felt that he needed more of it now, just to make him feel normal, and still enjoyed the relaxed feelings it gave him. He entered the house, going to his study where he'd left a little heroin, premixed and ready. Sitting in his chair he placed it on some foil and heated the foil underneath using a disposable lighter. The liquid warmed as Frank waited expectantly with his little glass tube and the fumes rose. He inhaled deeply, chasing the fumes, as the liquid ball rolled around the foil, the drug enveloping his senses, cuddling them in its insidious embrace. He drifted into semi-unconsciousness, his mind hazed from the effects of the drug. He stumbled to his feet and headed out of the door towards the kitchen, opening the fridge, to reveal a half drunk bottle of Lucozade, which he drank from the bottle. The effects would wear off in a minute as it'd only been a small amount. He walked to the bedroom and lay on his super king sized bed for ten minutes before changing into a grey T-shirt and jogging pants. Then he ran a cold sink of water and dunked his head into it, feeling the cold prickling his scalp. Hair dried with a towel, he brushed his teeth in a vain attempt to eradicate the bitterness from his mouth.

The intercom from the gate buzzed; Frank knew it would be Sheila who knew his security codes and would let herself in. He went to the front door and left it ajar to aid her entry to the house. *Always the gent,* he thought to himself, before walking to the kitchen and retrieving a can of Stella from the fridge. Now in the lounge, he spread out on the sofa and flicked on his seventy-five inch Smart television and was greeted with yet another playing of The Lord of the Rings.

"Bloody hobbits," he murmured and changed the channel to be greeted by news coverage of "bloody" Tim Peake.

"Hiya Frank, it's only me," yelled Sheila from the hall.

"Hi Sheila, kitchen and lounge please. There's half a bottle of white in the fridge. Help yourself."

Frank heard Sheila walk to the kitchen and the fridge door open. She always liked a glass of something when at his, no matter what time of day! Music started playing in the kitchen, where Sheila would have started work. Frank hopped the channels, settling on a run of Game of Thrones, where he could at least fantasise over some of the actresses, which also made him wonder what Sheila had on today. As if summoned, in she strolled, duster and polish in one hand, half a glass of white in the other.

"I'll just polish around here first, then hoover, if that's OK?"

"Fine by me," replied Frank, looking Sheila up and down. Sheila wasn't the typical looking cleaning lady and today was wearing a tight mini skirt and an open necked shirt revealing her cleavage. Her hair was tied back with a red neckerchief. Placing the glass down, she started polishing, Frank's eyes following her around the room, undressing her. He didn't think he could ask for a better cleaner and sat there getting his cheap thrills, wondering what lingerie she was wearing underneath.

"Fancy checking out the bedroom with me when you're done?" he asked hopefully, his speech slightly slurred.

"Oh Frank, bless you," Sheila looked at him, "you look the worse for wear. Not today love, I've got something on after this. I'll take a bottle of wine though and think of you later, when I'm relaxing in bed."

"Help yourself," he replied, always expecting the knock back. "Maybe another night?"

Sheila withdrew from the room and secured a couple of bottles for herself then returned to the living room with a hoover, where Tyrion Lannister appeared to be getting berated by Jamie. She plugged in and whipped round the room, still being watched by Frank. "That's me done darling," said Sheila, wrapping up the hoover cord. "I'll be back next week." She exited the room, packed the hoover away and left with her goods. Frank sat in the room, almost nodding off.

\*\*\*

The wind was whipping around the streets and rain

clouds threatened a deluge as a man wearing a Rockport coat sat observing 119 Palmerston View. Wellbury had just looked out of his front window and had partially shut the curtains, so he was in. Well, this would be the last time that he was in, this night would see the final breaths of a lazy, arrogant man who had bullied his way through life and who had little to offer to anyone. A business had been bequeathed to him by fine parents, both of them truly knowing that he didn't deserve it. He hadn't treated either of them kindly but love can be blind, especially where offspring were concerned, and being the only son, it was the only thing to do. Frank did not particularly treat anyone well and his drink driving and dirty little drug habit would get someone else killed before it did him. The police would do nothing and it was about time someone did.

The male tapped his pockets ensuring that the small blade was handy if needed, the other pocket holding a liquid filled syringe. With luck, the blade wouldn't be needed, the drug administered earlier, combined with any heroin taken should have dulled him enough. Latex gloved hands remained in coat pockets as the man moved forward, hood up and pressed the intercom.

"Who is it?" replied a drug slurred voice

"Joe."

"It's bloody late. Come in."

A buzzer sounded and the male entered the drive, head down, unsurprised by the stupidity of Wellbury allowing him onto the drive at this late hour. This was the dangerous bit. Approach calmly and keep in control, this fool deserves it. Heartbeat increased, as adrenaline flowed causing a tenseness within his body. Blue shoe coverings placed on just out of CCTV view. He approached the door, which was opening. Luck played its part. Frank had opened the door, turned away and entered a room to his right. The male waited, then entered and turned right.

Frank sat in his office behind a desk, foil and tooting tube in hand. Fumes inhaled and he slumped back discarding the foil and tube on the carpet. His eyes glazed as he attempted to focus on the male.

"Is that you ..."

Moving quickly forward, syringe now in hand, the male removed the cap with his teeth. Wellbury slumped, arms open, attempting to talk, attempting to focus, drool trailing from his mouth. Needle moved forward to his antecubital fossa.

"You'll feel a sharp prick," said the male smiling, emptying the full contents of the syringe into Wellbury's vein. Wellbury's eyes focussed in recognition, then glazed and closed.

"Then you'll feel nothing ... ever again!!!" finished the male, checking the carotid pulse, which faded and died. Adrenaline still high, the male produced socks from his pocket and shoved them deep into Wellbury's mouth, a little clue for the investigators. Now to finish the job, he needed to get away. Wellbury's head had slumped forward.

Job done, the male traced back his steps heading to the back of the house. The rear garden paths were gravelled and though footsteps would be noisy, they would leave nothing forensically, if he was careful. A rear gate secured from the inside led to a small paved alley which exited onto an adjoining street, where there was no obvious CCTV. The male thought, *keep it simple*. Wellbury allowed him in the front door. He could let himself out there as long as he had his hood up. Turn right to the back paths and away. CCTV at the house would just have him exiting the front door and not see him again.

A last look in the study confirmed he'd left nothing behind and out he went. The male walked casually from the rear alleyway, a good night's work done and disappeared on the south side of town. A call would be placed shortly and the fun would begin.

# Chapter 13

Matthew and Rachel stood in their kitchen having a cup of coffee before Matthew drove Rachel in to work. They had both spent a pleasant evening together and felt much closer. Matthew was going to open the shop up today, check all his stock and contact the accountant to ensure that all his books were in order. Rachel would have another busy day on the enquiry, seeing what she could do to progress the investigation today.

"I've been having a think," started Matthew.

"Go on," Rachel looked at him.

"I saw you were reading that Picoult book. You know the one where the lad ends up in prison dead with the socks. Do you not find that a bit weird?"

"What do you mean?"

"Well, you know, it's a strange way to die. Not that I'm an expert, but I've never heard of it before."

"So, what are you saying?"

"It's a bit lame," he looked at her sheepishly, "but I suppose what I'm saying is, do you think that your killer has read the book? Is that a line of enquiry for you? Has he left it on purpose as a clue for you? Left as a challenge to you?"

"Matt, you know that I can't talk to you about the case, but thanks for your thoughts," Rachel replied, smiling at him. "Now, I need to get to work." Matthew smiled back, both put their coats on and jumped in the car, enjoying each other's company on the trip. Pulling up to the rear of the station, Rachel opened the door, leant over and kissed Matthew's cheek.

"I'll see you tonight love," she stated.

"Yes, can't wait," he replied.

Rachel climbed out of the car and prior to closing the door, leant back in.

"It's not a bad thought Matt," she responded to his earlier comment "just one thought though."

"Yes?"

"You said 'he' when you mentioned the murderer. What makes you think it's a man?" she asked.

"Well, I suppose that it always seems to be a man. There never seem to be many female killers out there," he shrugged his shoulders.

"OK" she replied, "have a good one," and with that, shut the door and walked into the police station.

Matthew was happy with himself. He'd given Rachel something to think about, something that may help her. He was intrigued. *Was there anything he could do to help?* He was a bookseller of course, one of only two in the town. Then there was the library of course and the internet. If the killer had read the book, then the possibilities of them borrowing it, or buying it were immense, a needle in the proverbial haystack. He parked in town and walked onto the precinct, now eyeing people suspiciously. It could be any of this lot, any one of them walking around the town with not a care in the world, apart from the fact that they'd murdered someone. Joe said that Fatty was on heroin. It could be a user, or a supplier that he owed. It could be someone that Fatty had 'pissed off', let's face it, there would be enough of them, but why the socks? They had to have some significance. Matthew wasn't any detective but he was a man with time on his hands to do some research, it couldn't do any harm and would give him something to do.

Matthew approached the shop and went through his opening up procedure. The alarm silenced and the shop ready, he turned round his opening sign and stuck the kettle on. Business would probably be slow today but may pick up tomorrow for the weekend. He sat down at the counter and rang his accountant, who was satisfied that things were OK. Business was slow at this time of the year but would pick up at Easter. The shop made most of its profit on the run up to Christmas with gifts being bought for friends and family. The Christmas period profits usually saw Matthew through the leaner times of January, February and March. Although staying afloat, the shop was never going to make Matthew a fortune but with a well-paid partner and no kids, there was no problem paying the rent and bills. Matthew settled down behind his computer and contemplated how to start his self-styled investigation of the demise of Mr Frank Wellbury.

Logical steps were the key, he was sure, so he'd start with his own shop. Getting up from his seat, he walked over to the shelves to check fiction. All alphabetised and searching 'P' he found it; he had a copy of Jody Picoult's 'Nineteen Minutes' on the shelves. So, he had a copy and the library had a copy - he'd looked at it the other day. Just like he'd thought, this wasn't going to take him anywhere quickly. He picked out the shop copy, checking the back cover and the pages, noting that there was some wear to the soft corners. Probably needs replacing, he thought. Matthew made the assumption that all real book lovers wanted a copy that was in pristine condition and he would expect that himself. This one could go in his next sale and he'd knock the price down. Checking the spine, he saw that it too was worn, a crease running down the length of it.

"Someone's been reading this," he said out loud to himself. In itself that wasn't too strange but the rules in his shop were 'if you read it then take care of it'. Was it a coincidence with this book? Matthew walked back to the counter carrying the book. So, if someone's been reading it, they must have handled it. In realisation, Matthew dropped the book on the counter as if it had burnt his hands.

"Fingerprints," he said out loud again. The doorbell sounded and two old ladies shuffled into the shop.

"Morning," they both said in unison, ignorant of Matthew's failure to reply as they moved to the shelves. Matthew reached under the counter for one of the shop's paper bags and using his elbow manoeuvred the novel into it feeling a little ridiculous, though excited too. It was far flung, but the killer may have touched this. He looked up, seeing the pensioners, "Morning ladies, if you need any help just give me a shout."

"We're fine, dear," replied one. "We're just having a little browse before the library opens."

Matthew smiled at their inconsiderate comment, sipped his coffee and considered his next steps, turning to his computer. The computer held details of all of his stock, sales and purchases and a customer database. He entered the author into the search engine, which produced a list of all novels she had written and all formats that they had been produced in. 'Nineteen Minutes' sat within the list; highlighting it produced an image of the book on the screen. Interrogating the system, Matthew could see that he had purchased three copies in total during the previous six months. He had one copy in the shop and one copy at home, so that meant that a further copy had been sold. The system held all dates of sales so Matthew could see that the missing copy had been bought on the nineteenth of September 2015. Next to the record of this sale was a ticked box indicating that it was sold as a customer order. Matthew's breathing quickened; this could be it. He pressed the button to see who the customer was and was confronted by a name ... Richard Greaves! Matthew reached behind him for a stool and sat, mouth open in shock.

***

Rachel walked into her office, dumping her bags on the floor, her mind still pondering Matthew's suggestion regarding the book. It was important in an investigation to consider all lines of enquiry, whether a long shot or not. She was due in a management meeting shortly, with Jones and Andy, where they would sit and review everything that they had, try to identify gaps and consider how they could progress the investigation. They were due a peer review at the beginning of next week. They wanted to ensure that they hadn't missed anything important which would make them look foolish and incompetent to the force supervisor who would review them. Although Jones' prime goal was to ensure that a murderer was brought to justice, he also didn't want to face any professional embarrassment, which may affect any future career prospects or promotions. Rachel picked up her notebooks and checked that all was OK in the main office, where the detective sergeants were maintaining the day to day work of the criminal investigation department. All was good, so she grabbed a coffee and headed upstairs.

Entering the main briefing room, she was greeted by Andy and Jones, along with Tommy, who managed all the actions and results within the enquiry. He would be able to help assist in their debrief, and also note any new actions generated as a result of this meeting. Formality aside, Rachel sat down.

"Morning guys, how are you all doing?"

Smiles and "fine" were the replies and they started.

"Right, let's start with our main suspect, Marsden," commenced Jones. "We've had him under surveillance, arrested and interviewed. He's now out on bail. Bailed to his mother's address I believe?" looking towards Rachel.

"Yes," she affirmed. "As expected, 'No reply' interview, obviously orchestrated by his solicitor Briggs. Not enough to get a charge on him of any sort. The search of his flat gave us little. Confirmation that he is a heroin abuser from burnt foil, citric and needles located there. Clothing indicates that he is probably living there but there's no real food or home comforts. He appears to be living hand to mouth. The most significant thing there was the Rockport coat, which we have seized and has been sent for forensic examination. He had some sort of argument with Briggs whilst in custody but we have no idea what about. Bailed as we agreed."

"Thank you, Rachel," stated Jones. "Where are we at with the CCTV at the house and surrounding areas?"

Rachel again: "The subject in the Rockport is on Wellbury's CCTV entering the premises but is unidentified. We now have footage of the subject's exit, after we managed to sort out a glitch on our system. The subject exits shortly after attending but turns right towards the rear garden. There is a gate and alley at that location but no CCTV covering the rear path, gate or alleyways. Enquiries are still ongoing with any private CCTV at houses on the exit route but so far, no luck. The times that 'Rockport' is at the address are consistent with the pathologist's estimated time of death."

"Forensics?" asked Jones.

"I'll deal with them, Rach," stated Andy, "I was reading them all yesterday." Rachel smiled gratefully at Andy and took a sip of coffee.

"Firstly, the body. Obviously, you have both spoken with the pathologist. The reports are back from him and as indicated there was a disproportionate amount of "street heroin" in the blood, combined with alcohol indicating that the subject had been drinking. Also, they have found traces of an unknown drug within their samples. Work is ongoing to identify what the drug is, it's not commonly known to them or the significance of it clear." Jones looked up from his note taking.

"Is there a timescale for a result?"

"Maybe a week," replied Andy, continuing. "At the house, scenes of crime have lifted fibres, looked for footwear prints, taken fingerprint lifts, everything you'd expect. So they have the subject's prints and also a female's, as yet unidentified. Her prints are found on a wine glass in the kitchen, on the remains of the bottle in the fridge and on various surfaces. Obviously, CCTV puts the cleaner at the house that evening, she does not have a criminal record so we haven't a copy of any of her prints."

"Have we asked her for elimination fingerprints?" asked Jones.

"Not yet but it is set as an action," interjected Tommy.

"Good," replied Jones, with a quiet confidence that his team knew what they were doing.

"Continuing on, we have no fingerprints of our suspect Marsden at the crime scene. The socks found in the oral cavity have been seized as evidence. They look to be brand new and could have been bought anywhere. No significant other fibres as yet found on them. No footwear prints obvious within the hall except those that are matched by the victim's own footwear."

"Anything to add from you, Tommy?" asked Jones.

"No sir, all your policy is typed and submitted. We are on top of the actions and working flat out to get them completed."

"Good, thank you," he looked around, acknowledging everyone's efforts. "So, we have a suspect and we have him on bail. All the work is ongoing but we are still no further forward in proving or disproving that it was him.

We currently have no further suspects but we do have one further person of interest, Sheila Wilmslow. What are your thoughts about her, Rachel?"

"I think we need to consider how to move forward with her. She is present that night and we know that she has been in the house. She has no criminal history and there is no obvious benefit to her in killing Wellbury. There is nothing to indicate, so far, that she was aware of the subject's drug habit. We need to speak to her again and put more pressure on her to be totally honest with us. If she's been having an affair, we need to know. We need her fingerprints to eliminate from the scene and a consensual search of her house may be useful. We need to know more about her husband. If she is having an affair, has he found out and been to see the victim? He has a perfect excuse of working away, so could have travelled to Barnston and back to London without anyone knowing."

"Good, Rachel, good. We need to either have Wilmslow as a suspect or use her as a witness. Anything else?"

"The socks, Bob," said Rachel, "they are just out of place. Why do that? It seems that the victim has enough drugs in him to kill an elephant. They seem an unnecessary addition."

"True," replied Jones. "Go on, you've obviously got something to say."

"Well," started Rachel, feeling stupid, "I've just finished reading a book by an author called Picoult. A guy commits suicide in the book by stuffing a sock into his throat. It's a very particular and unusual thing to do. In the book the suicide guy had been bullied all his life. What if our murderer is emulating aspects of that death? Was Wellbury a bully? Are there unknown victims of his actions out there? We could start with the book. I know it's a long shot with the internet but we only have the library, Waterstones and Forseti's in town. Let's pay them a visit and see if they've sold it and if so, have records of who to?" Rachel had had her say. They'd either laugh or go with it. Jones looked at Rachel, clearly contemplating her words.

"All thoughts, Rachel, are up for consideration. It may also give us a legitimate reason to clear up your fellow's relationship with Marsden. We can interrogate his records, seize CCTV if possible. It may be a long shot but it would tidy up some loose ends."

"Right guys, we keep going. ABC, everything. Top priorities. Andy, chase those forensics. I want to know what the unknown substance is. Rachel, sort out the revisit to Wilmslow; we need to know everything she knows. If she won't play ball, then advise her I will have to consider bringing her in 'more formally'. Her voluntary interview should be at the police station. Let her have a feel what it's like to be brought in here, even if it's just as a volunteer. Rachel, please also allocate two detectives to start looking at Wilmslow's husband. Let's see how he features in all of this. If that requires a trip to the Met, then so be it. Tommy - enquiries at the bookshops, allocate a team to start them. Gold wants an update on where we are this afternoon, so let's see if we can give them some good news. Anything else?" he finished, looking around the officers who remained silent.

"Right, let's get to it." With that, the meeting was finished with everyone going off to see to their respective tasks.

*\*\**

Richard walked away from the train station having completed another shift at work, his day having been uneventful. His mood was sullen, with the weekend off before him and nothing to do. Another crap weekend for him; no friends to visit, family just bored the pants off him and the thought of spending any time with them drove him more into himself. He felt pathetic and couldn't spend the rest of his life upon the tedious treadmill that he walked in an unending loop. He wandered the streets, looking at people passing by, entering the pubs, laughing and joking, having fun, all ignorant of his life and none of them caring. Well, they would care if theirs was dramatically altered, a sudden death of a close one, an upheaval so horrendous as to bombard their senses to numbness. He'd like to see how they looked and felt then, how alone they felt in the world, where they would turn to.

"A killer's on the loose," he said, smiling to himself *and maybe next time it would be one of them*. They could join him in his own misery then at least he would know that others felt the pain that he did.

*\*\*\**

The door to the shop pinged and Matthew looked up. The shop was quiet, just Geoff having entered twenty minutes ago and sat at the back of the shop, take-out coffee in hand, reading a novel from the shelves. Matthew, still mentally perplexed and thinking about Greaves, looked at the males who had entered, both were wearing dark suits, clean shaven with short cut hair, and an air of arrogance about them. Matthew immediately thought 'cops' and smiling at them said, "Can I help you gentlemen?" The men scanned the shop and, noting it almost empty, approached the counter.

"Detectives Hall and Fisher from Barnston Police, sir and yes, we are hoping that you can." One of the males reached to his wallet and produced a plastic warrant card, passing it to Matthew. Matthew looked at it closely and handing it back said jokingly, "Is that real? It doesn't look real."

Detective Hall looked at it dejectedly, "Yes sir, it is. I know it looks cheap and nasty. People are always questioning it but that's what we get. Cutbacks, you know." He returned it to its wallet.

At the rear of the shop, Geoff's ears had pricked up at the conversation, though his head remained bowed, looking at the novel. The police in Forseti's on enquiries could be interesting. He stayed in position, waiting to hear the gossip.

"Anyway, what can I do for you?" asked Matthew.

"We're making some enquiries around bookshops in the town in relation to customers attending, books purchased and the like, so here we are."

"Yes," replied Matthew offering up nothing but fully understanding that Rachel must have listened to him. Exciting stuff!

"I can see from the shop that you sell everything here."

*Come on*, thought Matthew. *Spit it out or we'll be here for hours.* "Yes, this is a bookshop and I try to have as wide a collection as possible."

The detective looked at Matthew, weighing him up and trying to decide whether Matthew was taking the piss out of him. He carried on, "sir."

"Matthew is fine, detective. No need for formalities."

"Matthew, we're interested to see if you can give us some background on a novel you may have stocked; if you've sold it; if you have, who to. It is just a line of enquiry that we need to finalise in our investigation." Matthew looked at the detective, waiting for the book title. *Goodness, were all detectives like this?*

"And the book is?" asked Matthew.

"Oh yes, sorry. 'Nineteen Minutes' written by someone called Picoult."

"Let me have a look." Matthew checked his database for the novel for the second time that day. "Yes, here it is. My records show that I have sold two copies and have one currently in stock. I know one of them is at my house, I bought it for my partner, you see," he said in explanation. "The stock one I just put behind the counter, only yesterday I think, it's looking a little shabby." Matthew produced the book in its bag from under his counter. "The third sold to," he ran his finger across the screen "to a Mr Richard Greaves, some months ago."

"Greaves, you say. Is he a regular customer?"

"Fairly regular, although I did see him walking out of Waterstones the other day, so not as loyal as I'd like."

"Are there any other details about him on your system?"

"I usually just take a mobile telephone number, so the system can text the customer when their book order arrives in the shop. Yes, there it is." Matthew read the number out to the detectives who noted it down.

"Do you know anything else about him?"

"Not really. He's local. I went to school with him years ago, at Barnston School, but never mixed with him much."

"And the book on the counter there, you said it was a bit shabby. What do you mean?"

"Oh that. The corners are damaged slightly and a crease down the spine, you know like someone's been reading it."

"And do you allow customers to read in the shop?" asked the detective looking to the back of the shop where an old man was reading, answering the question really.

"Yes, but I would expect them to look after the book. I

can't sell this as new now."

The detectives looked at each other, and almost in unison stated, "Do you mind if we take it? You know, for reference. You can get it back later when the investigation is complete."

"By all means," replied Matthew.

"Just in relation to your customers Matthew, are you busy at the moment?"

"Not really, it's usually quiet at this time of the year."

"I thought I saw a young lad called Marsden walk in here the other day, a bit of a wrong un, if you know what I mean."

"Ah, Joe, you mean. Yes, Joe pops in from time to time. He's an old friend from school who I give a cup of coffee to now and then. He's a good lad with a bad habit. I'm sure you know what I mean." The detective didn't reply, just scrutinised Matthew.

"Does Marsden ever come in here to read, has he ever nicked from your shop?"

"Read? Possibly have a look round if I'm busy with a customer. Nick from me, never. We're still good mates."

"Thanks for your time, Matthew, you've been really helpful. We'll look after this," picking up the book. "You're Rachel Barnes' partner, aren't you?" the detective asked.

"Yes, that's me. Partner to Detective Inspector Barnes," Matthew smiled at the officers, "send her my regards, gents."

"Will do, Matthew. Take care, we may be back to see you again if we need to." The officers walked away towards the shop door and exited, heading off to their next enquiry at Waterstones. Matthew sighed in relief, thinking that it all seemed to have gone OK.

"Intrigue within Forseti's," stated Geoff who had walked up quietly from the rear of the shop.

"Well, not really I suppose. Who knows?" replied Matthew.

"Didn't realise that you were married to a police lady," stated Geoff. "She's heading up that murder investigation, isn't she? I read her name in the paper."

"She is indeed," beamed Matthew, "and I'm confident she's going to catch him."

"Well, let's hope so," replied Geoff, heading for the door. "Good luck to her and a good day to you." Geoff raised his hand in goodbye and left the shop. Matthew checked his watch, twelve midday and lunch time. He went to the shop door, turned the sign over, indicating he'd be back in thirty minutes, and locked the door behind him as he walked into town for some fresh air.

***

Sheila walked towards her car, having completed her last cleaning job of the day and climbed into the driver's seat. She sparked up a Marlborough, menthol of course, and checked her phone. No messages received from Seb. Well, she was getting her hair and nails done this afternoon, so he'd better not let her down. Opening WhatsApp, she flicked Seb a message:

*Are we still on for tonight gorgeous? x*

*Yes, I can't wait. Six o'clock at mine? x*

*You bet. I'll be there on the dot x*

Meeting confirmed, Sheila headed off to the beauticians to spoil herself; Seb was in for a treat tonight.

## Chapter 14

Sebastian walked out of his office after a hard day's work completing paperwork behind his desk. He'd be heading for the lakes tomorrow afternoon to spend some time with the family but first, a bit of Friday night fun with Sheila. He felt no regrets or remorse for his adulterous behaviour but instead felt that he had one life and he intended to live it. After all, he earned the money and kept his family well provided for. If he wanted some extra fun on the side then that was his prerogative. He checked his watch and got his iPhone out. Marsden better remember their deal. He sent him a text.

*Remember our arrangement. See you soon*

The phone indicated that it had been delivered; he didn't expect a reply, as he took a stroll through the precinct, heading towards the south of the town. Unbeknown to Briggs he was being watched.

***

Today Briggs would suffer some suitable recompense for his underhand dealings and adulterous lifestyle. The cyclist, pushing his bike at the head of the town, watched Briggs exit the business and head off after sending a message on his phone. The cyclist, having had confirmation that Briggs was still in town, headed off to make sure that he was ahead. The light was fading so conditions should be good. The message was a risk though, what if Briggs had a meeting arranged? If he wasn't alone then he'd have to walk away and deal with him another day. There wasn't any rush, there was all the time in the world and this could just be treated as a dry run. The cold clinical mind cycled towards the address on Mount Way, towards the stash location where necessary equipment was stored.

\*\*\*

Briggs closed in on the planned meeting location that he had made with Marsden but could see him nowhere. The little crook wasn't going to try and get one over on him, was he? Surely he wasn't that stupid. He held Marsden's liberty in his hands and didn't think Marsden was stupid enough to challenge him. He checked his phone, still no message and stood waiting. In a moment of clarity, he realised that of course he wouldn't reply, the police had seized his bloody phone. Briggs put his hand to his head. Damn, he shouldn't have sent the text that was delivered to Marsden's phone. The police had clearly left it switched on and would get to read the message. A bit of analytical work would identify Briggs' phone as the sender. He'd have to lie to them, pretend it was a meeting about the case, though up here that would look strange. He looked around, paranoia sneaking in. There was no one around, just a couple walking one hundred metres away. He'd better move away, it was too risky here, he'd deal with Marsden another day. He headed for home, looking around him all the time, to see if he was being followed. Maybe the police knew of his arrangement, especially if Marsden had said something in an attempt to save his skin.

\*\*\*

Briggs' home address was in darkness as the cyclist

approached it on foot. He had stashed his bike in an adjoining street ready to head off. The drive had laurels and a couple of rhododendron bushes which obscured the front door from a roadside view. There was no CCTV here and Briggs had forgotten to put on his outside lights. The environment was set and the cyclist stood relaxed beside a tall laurel which stood adjacent to the front door. The cyclist's position gave a clear view of the approaching drive and the door, perfect for tonight's task. He stood there ready, cosh in hand, syringe in pocket and a blade. A concealed bag lay beside the rear summerhouse, a change of clothes within. The blade would be needed tonight. A calm sereneness stilled the mind and body of the man. He waited.

***

Briggs whistled as he entered his driveway and the safety of his own property. He walked slowly up the driveway smiling, he appeared relaxed. His steady footfall led him towards the front door as he reached into his pocket pulling out his house key, placed it in the lock and turned.

The cyclist moved. Swiftly from the laurel he pounced. Cosh raised in his hand and Briggs turned.

'THWACK!' The cosh collided with Briggs' temple. His eyes dazed. Momentum drove both men onwards. The door crashed back. Briggs hit the parquet floor face first. The attacker landed on Briggs' back, knees pinning him. The cosh, driven with force into the base of the skull. Briggs groaned. Needle out, cap removed, contents emptied in the jugular.

Briggs couldn't move, then his brain exploded. The weight lifted off him as he felt his head pulled back by

171

his hair. All he heard was "corrupt cheat," as a scalpel blade passed before his eyes and opened his throat. His life bled away.

The cyclist stood, out of breath but calm. He'd have to move quickly. A mirror adorned the right wall of the hallway. Smashed with the cosh, he took a large shard of glass and used it to hide the clean cut of the scalpel in Briggs' flesh. He then placed it in Briggs' hand, careful not to stand on any of the pooling blood. That was enough. He backed out of the house pulling the door shut with a crooked elbow as he did so, his latex gloves bloodied. He walked towards the summer house, hands raised like a prepped surgeon, his covered footwear leaving no clear marks on the drive. Beside the summerhouse, his prepared tarpaulin lay. He stripped naked, his skinny body pimpling in the cold, rushing adrenaline warming him internally. All clothes in the tarpaulin and put a fresh set of clothes on. The tarpaulin wrapped and placed in a dark backpack, he checked back at the drive. Nobody around him, he walked calmly out of the entrance towards his bike, an unseen ghost in the night. Luck had stayed with him as before and another waste of a skin was disposed of in society.

Retrieving the cycle, the male cycled calmly through the cliff paths which would lead him to the sea. There he would take his used clothes to his pre-planned location and burn it all. The cosh he would throw in and once the fire burnt out, the beautiful water would remove all the traces that he had even been there. The bike could be dumped anywhere and would probably be nicked by some needy individual.

\*\*\*

Sheila climbed out of a taxi that had just dropped her

off outside of Sebastian's house. She tottered on the pavement in her high heels, waving goodbye to the driver as she went. Seb must have forgotten to switch the outside light on for her, so using her phone torch she negotiated the driveway with small unsteady steps, arriving at the front door in one piece. She straightened her body hugging dress and her hair and reached to the lock with the key that she had been given for gaining access for cleaning. Quick purse of the lips and flick of the hair she turned the key, opened the door and... screamed! A body lay on the floor. Sheila flicked on the hall light and screamed again. The body was Seb, lying in a pool of blood. Her scream pierced the air reverberating in the hallway.

"Oh my God, oh my God!" She moved forward and knelt next to him, her handbag falling into the viscous burgundy liquid. Reaching forward to his head, she looked for signs of life, the jagged tear to his throat obvious. Now, with blood on her shaking hands, she reached for the hall phone. Dropping the receiver, which spattered the congealing blood, she retrieved it and dialled 999, her gasping breath audible as panic threatened.

"Emergency, which service?"

"I need an ambulance. He's dead!" she screamed down the receiver, a bloody smear now on her cheek. Tears started smudging eyeliner as Sheila tried to control herself. The Ambulance Service call responder tried to calm her with no joy, only able to get the address from her before Sheila dropped the phone, arms encircling her body in protection. Already on the edge, she shrieked painful incoherence and held tight.

Sirens penetrated her mind and a car screeched to a halt on the driveway, Doors closed then the sound of running feet to the door which was pushed open gently by a black gloved hand.

"Jesus Christ," said a male voice whose uniformed body appeared in the doorway. The police had arrived first. The male turned behind him and spoke.

"One dead male and a female covered in blood. Hold the ambulance crew back, I'll check for life. Cover me from the door." Another officer appeared in the doorway as the first carefully approached Briggs.

"Now lady, I'm just checking him. You stay there," he directed her. Sheila didn't move. The officer checked visually, which was enough to determine death. He looked at the woman and nodded to his colleague, who approached her cautiously.

"If you can come this way, please Madam," said the officer, gently taking Sheila's arm, leading her away. Another police car had arrived outside, a police sergeant exiting.

"What have we got, officer?"

"A dead male inside with his throat cut. This female was sitting on the floor, beside him, with blood on hands and face." The Sergeant peered through the door, recognising Briggs and told the officer inside to exit and protect the scene. He turned to the woman.

"Madam, I am arresting you for suspicion of the murder of Sebastian Briggs. You do not have to say anything but it may..." Sheila didn't hear the caution as her legs gave way and she slumped to the ground, supported by the officer.

*** 

Rachel had just arrived at home after a long shift when her mobile telephone rang. Checking the display, she saw that it was Bob Jones. She looked at Matthew apologetically.

"It's the boss. I'll have to take it."

"Fine," replied Matthew, "I'll get on with dinner." Rachel pressed accept on the phone.

"Hi boss, what can I do for you?"

"Rachel, we've got another one."

"Another one?"

"A murder, Rachel, another bloody murder. The deceased is Sebastian Briggs."

"What?"

"Yes, and uniform has arrested someone. They've got Sheila Wilmslow in custody now." Rachel sat down on a kitchen chair with Matthew watching her closely.

"You OK, Rach?" he asked concernedly. Rachel ignored him.

"I need you in, Rachel. I'll meet you at the nick."

"Yes boss, there as soon as I can." The call terminated.

"I'm fine Matt," said Rachel, as he placed a hand on her shoulder. "It's work. I'm going to have to go back in. There's been another murder."

"Bloody hell!" he replied. "I'll drive you in. You can grab a sandwich, and a drink at Sainsbury's and make any calls on the way in."

"Cheers," replied Rachel, starting to get her brain into gear. She rang the office and told them she'd be in shortly. She wanted any free detective at the office to meet her there and Andy Burrows to be called in if he hadn't been already. Also, an immediate bail check on Joe Marsden, she needed to know if he was at home, where he had been tonight and who with. Matthew overheard everything but she'd have to trust him, she'd had the update from the detectives who'd visited him today. If this was the life of a Detective Inspector, she wasn't sure how long she could ride the rollercoaster without burning out. Rachel got into the car with Matthew.

"Bloody hell, this is exciting," he said, gunning the engine.

"Probably not the best time to joke about it, Matt. Somebody is dead."

"Fair enough," he replied, calming down, "let's get you in."

The journey into work was busy. A detective at the scene explained brief circumstances, Marsden was at home when they got there, Andy wanted a quick update, control room wanted confirmation she was en route. Matt had stopped at Sainsbury's and ran out, collecting food and drink for her. He pulled up behind the station and dropped her off.

"Good luck, Rach. Just ring me, whatever time you finish, and I'll come and get you." Rachel kissed him on the cheek, grabbed the orange Sainsbury's bag and entered the nick, leaving Matt to drive home.

Having entered she went directly to CID, where she knew that Jones would have found a desk. He sat there in his suit, looking at a computer screen, head rising as Rachel entered.

"Thanks for coming in, Rachel."

"That's OK, boss, what have we got?"

Jones told Rachel as much as he knew, describing the circumstances of how Briggs had been found and the current arrest of Wilmslow.

"I don't need to tell you how bad this is, Rach. The Chief is already breathing down my neck. We need to work fast to see if it's connected to ours, whether it is the same offender. Wilmslow's been arrested as she was there, but she rang it in, why would she do that? It was a male who rang the police about Wellbury's. I'm not convinced it's her but we have to go with what we have."

"I've had uniformed officers do a check at Marsden's. He was there and his mum says he's been there all afternoon, if we can believe that."

"OK," replied Jones, "I've got the on-call DI down at the scene with SOCO. Pending any different instructions from the Chief, we're going to let him keep the initial investigation with oversight by ourselves. We're here to help him, if he needs it, I'll take overall SIO responsibility for both, but leave you on the Wellbury case only, unless we find a link." Jones described the scene to Rachel. "The scene's a mess so I don't want you down there. I need you and Andy to review any developments from today and get priority actions ready for first thing tomorrow. We need to get moving on this, Rach. If this turns out to be the same suspect then we don't want a third one. That is not going to do either of our careers any good!"

"I'll head upstairs to meet with Andy," replied Rachel, unsurprised that Jones seemed more worried about his career than with the death of a member of the public. Heading upstairs, she heard footsteps rapidly approaching and found Andy puffing his way up.

"Why did they have to stick my office on the top floor?" he groaned. "Come on, Rach, I'll get the coffee on."

Coffee in hand, they both sat down to review where they were and updated each other on what they knew. Briggs' body had been removed from the scene and was on its way to the mortuary where the autopsy would be performed. The crime scene was secure and Wilmslow's house had a police guard on and had been "locked down" pending a full search tomorrow. They had established that Marsden had been at home for most of the day and at the moment had nothing to refute that. The report that had been prepared by the officers that visited Wilmslow previously had been completed and would be provided to her interview team. Until things developed within the new investigation there was nothing else of use that the inspectors could think of to assist. As instructed, they needed to review today's work.

"Right," started Rachel. "How did the enquiries go on at the bookshops?"

"So, they have brought a new name into the enquiry, Richard Greaves. He's not really known to us. Currently we have no address, no image of him but we have got a mobile telephone number. Apparently, he's the only customer who has bought a copy of Picoult, apart from Matthew, from Forseti's. It may be nothing. Matthew was very helpful and also gave us a copy of the book from his shelves. He said it looks as though it's been read - creased spine, damaged corners etc. We've seized the book for prints."

"We need to find out more about Greaves."

"Matthew said that he knew him from school, so he's a local. We have a mobile and a starting point at the school. Also, he said he'd seen him in Waterstones the other day and given an approximate time and date."

"Right," said Rachel, who had been jotting notes down. "Priority actions tomorrow to start with: Full intelligence picture on Greaves; I want billing applied for on his phone for the past three months; housing checks - we need to know where he is living; driving licence, passport... can we get an image of him? Priority to get everything we can from Waterstones. Can they tell us what he bought? Have they got CCTV which may have captured an image of him? All the usual checks, on Facebook, Twitter, Instagram etc.

"Got it," replied Andy.

"Now, as for Marsden, we need surveillance on him starting tomorrow morning. The authority is still in place so let's use it and see what he is up to. If you can put a call in to surveillance tonight and tell them we want them over here tomorrow? The book we've seized: I want that examined tomorrow for prints. Don't worry about any damage the dyes and powders may cause, Matthew can stand it. Am I missing anything?" finished Rachel, looking up at Andy, who was smiling.

"Not at all, boss," he replied, "you're definitely getting the hang of this. I'll get straight on with surveillance and have the actions ready for tomorrow."

"Thanks, Andy, and thank you," she replied to his compliment. Rachel started documenting all the actions required. The pathologist would have started on the autopsy and once done here, she'd go and find Jones and await the result. It was unlikely that Wilmslow would be interviewed tonight as there was too much to do for the investigative team. They'd want to be fully prepared for the interview with all the information they could get. Let's hope it is her, she thought, at least they'd have taken a murderer off the streets.

***

An hour later, Rachel found Jones sat within the same seat, writing policy decisions within his book.

"Wilmslow said nothing on arrest and has said very little in custody," he updated her, "if anything, they are saying that she seems to be in total shock. She's getting assessed by a force doctor to ensure she's mentally fit to be detained and interviewed. Who knows if she's done it, or them? If she hasn't, then she's the unluckiest woman alive at this moment in time." Rachel updated Jones regarding her proposed actions, which he agreed with. "If you can type them up, Rachel, and submit them, I'll document our conversation and decisions in the book first thing tomorrow." Jones' phone rang.

"Jones."

"Hi, Raheel, just wait a minute, I'll stick you on hands free," Jones laid his phone down, loudspeaker on. "You've got me and Rachel Barnes, Raheel, speak freely." Raheel Nazar was the duty Detective Inspector.

"Boss, Rachel. I've just walked out of the preliminaries of the autopsy to give you an update."

"Go on," cut in Jones, impatiently.

"The pathologist is confirming another murder sir. He's basically said that it's been manufactured to look like suicide but he doesn't believe it to be so." Jones and Rachel sat back, listening intently.

"The victim has bruising to the base of his skull and to his temple which is believed to have been caused by a blunt instrument. This could have been done to disorientate or immobilise the victim, the damage to his face an indication that he hit the floor with little attempt to protect his fall with hands or arms. The front of his hairline is "ripped", indicating his head pulled forcibly back. The long ragged laceration to his throat disguises the start of a clean cut from left to right. The left side cut is thin and penetrative, the pathologist believes caused by a blade. The victim held a large piece of mirrored glass, damaging his palm but there are no further cuts elsewhere on his hands. For your information, forensics recovered shards of glass from the back of the clothing the victim was wearing. They think that the mirror was smashed after he was already assaulted."

"OK, Raheel, anything else so far?"

"Yes sir, the clincher. The pathologist believes that there is a pinprick and bruising to the side of the neck, which is indicative of an injection site."

Jones looked at Rachel.

"Sir, it's possible that whoever murdered Briggs did Wellbury too"

"OK, Raheel, thanks for the update. I'll see you back

here when you are done there."

"Yes, sir." The call was terminated.

"Right, Rachel, the pressure is really going to start mounting on us now. That's two murders connected by the probable injection of a drug. He or she is escalating. Look at the violence used this time. We cannot have another one." Jones looked directly at Rachel and continued, "This one will be high profile and the press will be all over it. You and I are going to do the press conference in the morning. Make no mistake, Rachel, if we don't get this sorted fast, our organisation will feed us to the lions and bring in someone else."

"The priority has to be to sort Wilmslow out in custody, sir."

"Yes, but do you really think that it's her?"

"Being honest, no. I'm hoping it is, because it would make this investigation easier, but I doubt it."

"Me too," replied Jones, "so we maintain focus. Wilmslow we can now deal with over the next twenty-four hours, so we concentrate on Marsden and this Greaves character. Get your actions scripted up for me and then get off home. Raheel has just joined our team. I'll sort priorities with him tonight and then see you both in the morning."

"Sir." Rachel stood and left the room, returning to the intelligence cell. She texted Matt to collect her. She'd have written everything up by the time he landed.

Twenty minutes later, Rachel walked out of the back of the nick to be met by Matt, who drove them both home. Entering the house, he stuck the kettle on for a coffee.

"So, big press conference this morning for you, DI Barnes" said Matt cheerfully. "BBC, ITV and the like will be there, your face on the big screen. You terrified?"

"Bloody right I am," Rachel replied, accepting her

coffee. She had told Matthew about the press conference on the journey home.

"So," started Matthew, "what's really going on? What's the latest?" He drew out a kitchen chair for Rachel to sit on and sat by himself.

"Well, you know that I've checked out your theory about the book because the detectives have been to yours today."

"Yes, good theory, isn't it?" he beamed like a child.

"I don't know if it is or not. As you know, it's brought Greaves into the picture - a name for us to look at, so we will see."

"And tonight's victim?" asked Matthew.

"You'll hear first thing tomorrow on the news anyway," she paused, "Sebastian Briggs, a solicitor from town."

"You are bloody joking." Matthew sat back in his chair, nearly spilling his coffee. "I only saw him the other day. I sometimes see him in town. He came out of his office and headed up to the police station. Waved at some woman on the way."

"When was this, Matt? What woman?"

"A couple of days ago, I didn't know her. A brunette, who drove a red Corsa with Sheila's Maid advertised on the windows." Rachel looked at Matt.

"How come you've seen or know all these people, Matt?"

"I grew up here, Rach, I own a shop in town. I know loads of people. That's what happens in a small place that you've grown up in."

"We're probably going to need to get some witness statements from you, Matt. You do know that?"

"Yes, yes, not a problem," he replied casually, his mind ticking over "How was he killed?"

"Keep it to yourself?" Rachel had decided she had to

trust him. He was helping the investigation with his information from the shop. He was her partner, for Christ's sake.

"Throat cut with the glass from a mirror." He definitely didn't need to know everything, though. He looked at her.

"You're joking."

"No." He just sat there. "What's up?" He sat there silently. "Matt, what's up?" asked Rachel again, her voice raised in concern.

He stood up, then sat down, he couldn't settle, then leaned forward to Rachel, taking her hands.

"Now you're going to think me mad but hear me out. I've just finished reading a book by an author called Niederman. It's basically about a bent law firm. In the book, a lady kills herself. Rach, she does it by committing suicide using a shard of glass from a broken mirror. She cuts her throat."

"What?" said Rachel, bemused.

"It can't be a coincidence, Rachel. That's two murders using lines from a book. He's got to be using the stories to help him plan what he's going to do. Your murderer is finding books to help his research."

*What if he was?* thought Rachel, *what if Matt was onto something?*

"Tell me everything that you know about Richard Greaves, Matt."

Matthew trawled his memory and recalled as much as he could about Greaves' past.

# Chapter 15

Rachel sat within her office at her current 'home from home', ensuring that her actions from last night were all being allocated appropriately. The surveillance team were once again in the town and would start their day seeing what Marsden was up to. She wanted them to be behind him when the press conference went out. It was going out live, so any reaction that he had as a result was important to capture. Enquiries would start again at Waterstones as soon as they were open and a team were heading to the school to get what information they could on Greaves. She'd already submitted a confidential report about the information that Matt had given her about him last night. She'd sit down with the boss, Andy and Raheel afterwards and see what they should do with it. To her, Greaves was at least now 'a person of interest' and warranted surveillance behind him. As the clock ticked nine, Rachel walked downstairs towards the conference room where the press and cameras awaited. She wore her best suit and met Raheel and Jones in a small room next door, Raheel standing smartly in a suit and Jones in full dress uniform. The press liaison officer briefed all the officers: Jones would give the opening statement and Rachel would deal with investigative questions. Raheel would be there as her moral support and named as the DI investigating the most recent murder.

The officers stood waiting, all of them bricking themselves.

"It's time," said the press liaison, hand ready to open the door. Jones nodded at him. The door opened and led by Jones, they walked into the conference room.

Rachel was temporarily blinded as camera flashes exploded, together with the whirring and click of depressed buttons as photographs were taken. Reporters' voices immediately joined the cacophony as the officers walked towards three prepared lecterns.

The conference went as expected with Jones leading the way, advising the public that he had the most dedicated and experienced team who would stop at nothing to bring the offender to justice. Rachel couldn't help but feel like a 'fatted calf' as Jones introduced her to the press throng, knowing that if any heads rolled during this investigation, if it went wrong, then hers would be at the top of the list. She fended questions by different reporters, didn't commit to anything except to finalise the meeting by saying that she personally would ensure that the offender was brought to justice and that she was close to capturing him or her. The management team exited the room, press liaison closing the door behind them. Rachel felt tired out, her shirt sticking to her back with moisture.

"Well done everyone," said Jones with a smile on his face. "Brave though Inspector Barnes, you know, personally vouching that you'll catch him. Don't know if I'd have done that," he finished, smiling, in his mind knowing that if the investigation didn't progress, then Rachel would be the first to fall.

"We're going to catch him, sir. We're getting close. We just need some luck and to keep going at it. He'll come."

"Well, we'd better get back to it then. The clock is counting. I'll see you both upstairs after I've got changed in say, half an hour." The officers departed the room.

\*\*\*

"Quick love, come through here," Joe's mum shouted at him from the living room. Joe walked into the room where the television was on, picturing a senior police officer wearing uniform and two others wearing suits.

"There's been a murder, son, some sort of lawyer or something. In Barnston, I can't believe it." Joe looked at the television, where an austere looking copper wearing uniform was providing information to the press and public about the murder of Sebastian Briggs. That's why the police had called last night, to see whether he was in, they suspected him of this one too. He hadn't met Briggs as he had told him to, but instead thought he'd make him wait. Now with Briggs dead, who would he get to represent him? He watched the rest of the conference, where a woman in a suit stated that she was going to catch the murderer.

"Mum, I need to go out." Joe shoved some trainers on, grabbed his jacket and headed out of the door.

***

"All units, the subject is exiting the front door, through the gate and left towards the town."

The surveillance team were in position and ready to see what Marsden did as a result of the press release. Cars were ahead in the town to pick him up and a couple of officers would follow him on foot. The team had learnt from last time and were prepared with push bikes too. He wasn't going to lose them easily this time.

Joe walked at a steady pace within the estate, nodding to a couple of people and heading for an address two roads over. Nearing the address, he checked around before entering the gate and knocking on the door. The street was quiet with only work vans and a couple of cars parked on the street.

"The subject is knocking at the door," an officer transmitted whilst sitting within a van. Luck was on their side as he just happened to be sitting in the right location.

"Front door is opened by a young male, in his

twenties, with cropped dark hair. Subject is having a conversation."

***

"Hey up, mate," said Joe, "I put an order in for an ounce of white. Won't be needing it now."

"No probs, Joe. I've got orders coming out of me ears, so I'll flog it elsewhere. Is everything OK?"

"Yeah, just a bit skint at the moment and can't afford it."

"Well, if you need a borrow of some cash with some interest added on, give me a holler."

"I'll be fine. See you." Joe turned and walked away. He had Briggs' money now and Briggs had no need for the coke. He walked to the top of the path and stopped, checking the cash he had on him.

***

"Subject is away from the door and stops at the gate. He's looking at something in his hands," The officer checked through binoculars. "He's counting cash, a few notes, placed them in his pocket, and he's away towards the town." Now away from the van's view, another operative would start following Joe as the rest of the team worked together to shadow him to his next location.

***

Joe arrived at the town centre. He was feeling spaced out today, not fully on his game. The last few days were taking their toll on him - he was tired and had the cops breathing down his neck. Thank God his name hadn't hit the press; he certainly wouldn't be able to walk out on the streets if it had. He'd kept his head down, not seen any associates and he didn't think that anyone knew, or cared, that he had been arrested. They would know his flat had been searched so might suspect, but he'd heard nothing. At least he'd been getting fed by his mum. He needed to sort his priorities. The town would now be crawling with cops and with the press. Scoring wouldn't be easy as the dealers would be being careful but he needed some today. He also needed to find another solicitor who'd represent him; he didn't just want a duty solicitor if the police hauled him in again. Would they? He didn't know. They had his phone so they'd know Briggs' number was in it; they'd no doubt heard them arguing in the nick. He was already on bail for murder and then the bloke who was representing him was murdered too. It looked bad for him. He looked around, paranoid that he was being watched, but there was nothing obvious. Joe approached the Big Issue seller.

"You heard the news?" Joe asked.

"Yes, mate, slippery Briggs, eh? Plenty of us would have liked to do him over but bloody kill him, that's heavy."

"Are they on? I've lost me phone."

"Yeah, Scousers are but they're being cagey. Changed location again, to down by the beach. A couple have said they're meeting down there at one."

"Cheers." Joe walked off, heading towards Forseti's. If he needed something he needed a friend and he knew that Matthew wouldn't let him down.

Matthew looked up at the door as a drained looking Joe walked through.

"Morning, Joe, I haven't seen you for a few days. What have you been up to?" Matt asked cheerfully, turning to the kitchen door.

"If only you knew," replied Joe, scanning the shop and seeing that there were no customers in the shop.

***

"The subject is in to Forseti's," commentated an officer.

"No need to enter. Control the shop doorway - we will take him away from here," stated the team sergeant. He had been briefed that there was no need to control the subject in this shop and could only assume that the investigation had other means of knowing what happened within there.

***

"Tell me all about it," replied Matt, handing Joe a welcome coffee. "Have you seen the news? Solicitor dead in town, murdered it appears. That's my lass on the telly," Matt beamed proudly.

"The one in the suit, heading the investigation?"

"Yep, that's her."

"You're joking!" exclaimed Joe.

"I'm trying to help her a bit, you know, mate, point her in the right direction, a bit of super sleuthing on the side of bookselling."

Joe looked at Matt, astounded.

"So, you're responsible for putting them on to me and getting me nicked?"

"What do you mean?"

"Don't 'what do you mean' me, you know what I mean. You know they've had me in for Wellbury's murder… they're probably after me for this one too. A mate?" Joe looked at him in disgust, drank his coffee, dropping the cup on the shop floor as he left, ignoring Matthew's protests behind him.

***

The intelligence team had been working non-stop since receiving Richard Greaves' name. They now had an address on the south side of town and a photograph from a provisional driving licence that he had applied for a couple of years ago. His banking records showed that he was in receipt of a regular wage paid by the NHS giving them another location where they could make enquiries. Officers attended the school, speaking to a couple of the older teachers who unfortunately recalled little about Greaves. He was remembered as being quiet and introspective, a loner who didn't have many friends. He was bullied a bit by the bigger lads but not believed to be anything serious. There were never any discipline and attendance issues that they could recall. Not a particularly bright or gifted pupil but he'd probably do OK.

Rachel sat with Andy and Raheel getting an update on him, on what was happening with Wilmslow and on how the surveillance was going. Wilmslow's interview was particularly informative. She appeared to be in such a state of shock that she was rambling a lot. The doctor had assessed her twice now and stated she was fit to be detained and interviewed. There were two constants in her narrative; one, she continually stated was that she knew nothing and was not a murderer and two, she clearly loathed her husband and blamed him for this whole mess. Her affair with Briggs she had admitted, stealing wine from Wellbury she admitted but the police had, so far, found no evidence to prove that it was her.

"She seems to be the wrong person, in the wrong place, at the right time," concluded Raheel.

"Anything on the husband?" asked Rachel.

"We've made all the enquiries that we can down there with no joy. It appears that on the night of Wellbury's death he was at a work function. CCTV in that area proves him to be there. Last night he was in London too, which is confirmed by Sheila, hence her arranged meet with Briggs. All his phone data puts him in London when the offences are suspected of being committed."

"Good, that's him out," replied Rachel. "How's surveillance going on Marsden?"

Andy reported back on his movements since the press conference. The team still had control of him and he was currently down at the beach hanging around. Other smackheads had been seen in the area, so it was likely that he was waiting to score.

"Right," replied Rachel, "so we have everyone controlled apart from Greaves. Who, if he is our murderer, is running around loose, doing who knows what? What are we going to do about him?" Both Andy and Raheel looked to her for guidance: she was the deputy SIO, after all.

"Fingerprints on the book? Where are we?"

"Marsden's aren't on it," replied Andy. "Your Matthew's are, no surprise there. There are a few inconclusive partial prints that won't help. However, there are another set of prints which are everywhere in the book but are unidentified. Meaning whoever has been reading the book has not been arrested by the police before - we don't have a copy of their prints."

"Do we have a copy of Greaves' prints?" asked Rachel.

"No."

"OK, enquiries at Waterstones. What have they brought up?"

"The officers have rung up ten minutes ago," started

Andy. "They've interrogated the CCTV at the store, the tills, the stock system. They believe that they have an image of Greaves entering and leaving the shop and also browsing in the store. He's changed a bit from the old driving photo we have but they say that it's a good likeness. The time and date match those given by Matt. Within the shop, he's browsing the crime/thriller section and selects an item and takes it to the till. The team is working with Waterstones now to see if they can pinpoint what it is. They'll ring if they get anything," he concluded.

"Just so I've got this clear," Rachel said, "Greaves lives alone on the south side, believed to be a bit of a loner with no real friends, a guy bullied when younger. Works for the NHS, though we haven't discovered in what capacity - that would possibly give him access to drugs. We have him in a bookshop but don't know what he has bought yet. We don't have his fingerprints. Is that about right?"

"Yes," both men replied.

"Have you added his name to the surveillance authority, Andy?"

"Yes, added and authorised for everything that we may need."

"Good. Let's get the prep work done to put surveillance on him. Observation points, plans etc. We'll divert the team from Marsden, who looks like he's going to score and probably sleep it off at home. Objectives for the team are as usual with priority of covertly obtaining a fingerprint. Enquiries to be made as soon as possible at the hospitals to find out what he does." Andy's telephone rang.

"Hello. Yes. Yes," he grabbed a piece of paper and wrote '*Andrew Niederman - The Devil's Advocate*', showing it to Raheel and Rachel.

"Does that mean anything to you?" Raheel asked Rachel.

"It certainly does."

\*\*\*

Richard sat in his flat, having watched the news with a satisfied smile on his face. *Briggs dead, well if there was any true justice in the world, then there it was. The arrogant man had got what he had deserved and the police looked like they were floundering in their investigation. Sure, they would stand there brashly announcing that they were making diligent enquiries and 'closing in' on their suspect but everyone knew that they would be in a mess. Two murders within a very short period in quiet little Barnston, they would be in chaos, trying to catch the culprit and prevent another one.* Another one would make three, giving the offender the title of a 'Serial Killer' - would make them the newest member of that club. The woman stood on the television like Jane Tennison, claiming that she would capture the villain.

"You wanna be careful," said Richard, talking to the image of her on the screen, "he may see that as a bit of a challenge." *Maybe the weekend wasn't going to be as boring and uneventful after all,* he thought, switching off the TV, grabbing his coat and heading out. He strolled nonchalantly down the path, feeling much happier in himself today. Maybe life was on the up for him, maybe today would see new events in his life, a new life unfolding in front of him. He found himself strolling towards Mount Way, just to have a peek to see what the cops were up to. As he approached, he could see a marked police vehicle blocking the driveway entrance with a young policeman standing next to it. A person wearing a white forensic suit was just exiting the driveway and walking towards a vehicle marked SOCO parked nearby, hands carrying clear bags containing items. How interesting, thought Richard, wishing to get a closer look. Intrigue overcoming his wariness, he crossed the road and headed on the footpath which would take him directly past the uniformed cop. Getting closer, he could see the white suit sitting within his van, drinking coffee from a flask.

"Sir, if I could just stop you there and ask you to cross back over the road, please. This is a crime scene."

"Is it really?" said Richard, attempting an educated accent, "is it the one from the television?"

"The television?"

"You know, the press conference from this morning. Sebastian Briggs, murder."

The officer looked confusedly at Richard.

"I couldn't say, sir, but it's definitely not an area you can hang around in. Are you from the press? What's your name?"

"No, not the press, officer, just a concerned member of the public."

"And your name sir?"

"Oh, never mind, officer, I'll be on my way." Richard hadn't counted on being asked questions.

"For the third time, your name?" the officer repeated more directly.

"John Greaves," replied Richard, giving his father's name, in panic. "I'll be on my way. Morning officer." Richard walked swiftly over the road and up the hill. Glancing back, he gave an acknowledgement wave to the officer whom he noted was writing something down on a sheet of paper. Richard negotiated the adjoining roads and wended his way to the cliffs, where he looked calmly over the North Sea, relishing in the freshness of the day.

At the crime scene, the police officer on cordon duties rang the intelligence unit and spoke to one of the detectives in the unit.

"Hi there, it may be something or nothing but I've just had a strange bloke snooping around at Briggs'. He gave me the name John Greaves then walked off in the direction of the cliffs." The call was quickly terminated.

\*\*\*

"Rich, it's Andy calling from Intell. A bloke called Greaves has just been visiting the crime scene. I don't know if it's our subject but he's headed towards the cliffs."

\*\*\*

"Rich to the team," transmitted over the radio, "Possible sighting of our subject on the south side of the town, heading towards the cliffs. All units, towards that location. Let's get an identification of him." The surveillance team moved as one unit towards the south side of town. Traffic was busy but they knew the town well, including the short cuts by vehicle and by foot. They would get to the cliffs and start combing the area for their man.

Greaves still remained looking out to sea when a surveillance operative first sighted him.

"Good possible on the footpath overlooking the cliffs," was transmitted. "I'll walk past and see if it's him." The officer parked his car and tracked back to where Greaves was still standing, planning his route to get a view of Greaves' face. He walked steadily up to Greaves, who looked around on hearing footsteps. The operative smiled at Greaves and wished him a good afternoon as he walked past. Greaves just smiled and looked back out to sea dismissing the man from his mind. *It was a great day, a great day to be alive.*

The operative continued walking in the same direction and at the next junction turned left out of view and transmitted on his covert radio.

"Sighting of the subject on the footpath overlooking the sea, approximately fifteen metres prior to the junction of Robe Street. The subject is wearing a grey waterproof coat, dark jeans and black trainers. He wears spectacles."

"Loud and clear and Jonny now has a view of the subject and has control," came a reply on the radio. The initial operative would use an alternative route back to his car and get in it when it was safe to do so. He would have to keep clear of the subject now as the subject had seen his face also.

Richard decided that he would take a wander into town, grab a coffee, something to eat and maybe have a look around the library or bookshops. With a spring in his step, he headed towards the town, unbeknown to him, followed by the surveillance team. There were a few people enjoying the day, though Richard preferred his own company and interacted with none of them. He'd decided to head to town via the sea front and on the approach could hear the chatter of the arcades. Out towards the beach a couple of wetsuit clad figures sat within the sea waiting for a suitable set of waves to make their attempts at surfing. On the beach, a family sat hunkered down in coats whilst their children enjoyed the breaking waves, screaming as they ran away from the incoming tide. Richard looked further up the bay towards the harbour and again unbeknown to him, 'Click'.

"Photograph obtained of the subject," transmitted on the surveillance airwaves. The operative stood next to a camper van which was parked in the harbour car park. She'd been there ten minutes, taking various photographs and blended into the environment. The zoom capability of her camera was outstanding, so although she had obtained the image, there was no way that Greaves could even see her. Her objective achieved, she returned to her vehicle.

Richard looked at the arcades as he walked past, their tired exteriors with flaking paint and glitzy lights depicting the 'Great British Seaside'. To Richard, there was nothing great about this town that he'd grown up in. There was actually nothing to keep him here. *Maybe he should move on, maybe move abroad. That would be great, a new life for Richard Greaves away from the entrapment that was Barnston.* He spotted a glint on the pavement and bending down, picked up a ten pence piece. Flipping and catching the coin, he thought, *Why not?* as he entered an arcade, approaching a penny shove machine. Checking each area, he selected one and chose the middle slot. Waiting until the machine retracted, he sent the coin down. *Perfect,* it settled on the tray at the front waiting for the mechanism to slide back again. He held his breath, there it went, the coin dropped perfectly, pushed forward towards waiting coins. Success!! Ten pence coins rattled into the front collection port. Richard smiled, scooping them up and counting them now as three pounds. Would his luck ever run out, what a terrific day he was having with lady luck on his side.

\*\*\*

Rachel walked into the intelligence unit to get an update.

"We're on Greaves, Rach," stated Andy. "As predicted, Marsden scored then went straight home." He updated Rachel as to what had happened at the crime scene and on how they had found Greaves. "The team have got an image of the subject," he continued, showing her the snapshot of Greaves on his computer screen. "They'll stay with him all day now and I've booked them for tomorrow too."

"Good stuff, Andy. He looks like nobody in that image, a grey man. Are you our murderer?" Rachel asked the image of Greaves, examining it closely.

\*\*\*

Richard climbed the hill to the town centre and headed straight towards Costa, entering the coffee house. He bought a hot chocolate with marshmallows and a flake and sat looking out of the window at the world passing by. The shop was busy and he had no reason to notice the old lady who took a seat on the table next to him, waiting for a coffee to be delivered. Under their notice board, Richard noticed they had a temporary charity bookshop and stood up to take a look. The usual romantic rubbish, a couple of westerns and some cookbooks stood spines outward with a mixed pile to the right. *What was that at the bottom there,* he thought, bending down and pulling out Robin Cook's 'Coma'. *That would do him, another film he'd seen but not read the book*. He'd take that for a quid, which he placed in the collection pot, returning to his table and flicking through the pages. The old dear had her coffee now and sat looking at the screen of a dated mobile phone, painfully pushing buttons and texting,

*Drink bought, charity book bought,* Pressing 'send', it went out to the team.

Richard finished his chocolate which he had enjoyed and with his book, left the shop.

After he had left, the old lady reached over with a Costa tissue and picked up Greaves' empty glass, depositing it into her voluminous handbag before sending out a text to her boss John.

*Fingerprints and DNA recovered.*

The old lady sat enjoying her coffee, listening to her team's radio transmissions as she enjoyed the warm, ambient atmosphere of Costa.

# Chapter 16

Sheila Wilmslow sat within her cell at the police station, wondering how her life could have taken such a downward spiral. She'd never been arrested in her life and apart from in the past few days, had not even had any interaction with the police. Now she sat in a blue jogging top and pants, staring at a metal toilet with no lid, surrounded by four walls and a solid steel door. Her personal loss of Seb was nothing compared to the inner fright and turmoil that she felt at her current situation. Her anger started to build. She'd done the best she could in the interview, told them everything she knew, which amounted to nothing, and was still sitting here. Her husband, bless his bloody soul, had sent up a lawyer from London when she rang him, saying he would be up himself as soon as he could. He still hadn't even bothered to appear. Sheila had done nothing and had been arrested for something she hadn't done. She'd had to be watched by some bitch policewoman when she showered and was being fed McDonald's crap. She stood up, walking towards the cell door. Where the hell had her husband got to? Where was the loser? She'd never even have been with Seb if she'd had a decent husband. She thumped the door with her fist, the serving hatch rattling.

"Let me out of here," she spoke, her other hand grasping her hair back, fingers entangling it. No answer.

"Let me out!" louder. Tears started, wetting already smudged eyeliner. "If he bloody wasn't away all the time," she spoke to herself.

She thumped the door then stepped back and kicked it, anger consuming her. Rage taking over, building in her body, hands shaking, she arched her back, head back and screamed, "LET ME BLOODY OUT OF HERE!" then ran at the door, head colliding on metal with a crack and

Sheila dropped to the floor unconscious, blood streaming down her face.

***

Matthew had spent the morning rearranging the goods and trinkets shelving section within his shop. Primarily a book shop, he had dedicated a small section where he sold book related items and a couple of word games. Boggle and Scrabble were always stalwarts in the shop, people seemed to like to buy them for presents for friends. He was partial to a bit of Bananagrams himself and sold a few of them with his spiel to parents about how good developmental word games were for their children. Various bookmarks, book lights, tea and coffee mugs adorned other areas. Footfall this morning had been light but he'd sold a few books which would help keep the bills paid. The two old dears who had enquired about the library the other day had returned to ask whether he sold second-hand books, so he pointed them to his sales section. Geoff had been perusing the shelves again but didn't stay to read and hadn't stayed for long. Parents with kids had been in and out and he'd managed to sell off another copy of 'The Philosopher's Stone'. His phone pinged as a text came in.

*Rachel – Hope all's OK love. You heard of a book called Coma?*

*Matthew – Robin Cook's the author. It's a thriller about illicit supply of human organs.*

*Rachel – OK. Thanx see you tonight x*

A cryptic question from Barnston's lead investigator; he'd find out more tonight. Rachel had mentioned Greaves to him last night. Sure, he was a strange lad at school but a murderer? He'd not been in the shop for a couple of days; *was he keeping his head down and out of the way?* Something had been niggling at Matthew's mind all morning about Wellbury,

something about the past but not school days, something else. Matthew checked his watch and saw that it was nearly lunchtime, time for a bite to eat. He picked up his coat and phone, grabbed his keys and departed the shop, putting up his lunch break sign, before locking the door and walking into town.

He walked towards the railway station and glancing up at its clock, checked the time against his watch. He'd grab a quick bite to eat from Thomas the Bakers and maybe a coffee from Costa. Maybe Rachel and him should take a train trip to Fenchurch sometime soon, go out for a nice meal, and have a stroll along the river. Matthew stopped outside Thomas' staring into the window... the train, Fenchurch, Wellbury. That was it, Wellbury had been involved with someone years ago, someone who had been involved in a tragic accident on the railway lines. It was in the papers at the time. He needed the library, as they would have a record of newspaper publications on microfilm. He walked into Thomas' and bought a ham salad baguette and an iced finger which he couldn't resist and headed to the library. Entering, he saw that it was fairly quiet and walked up to one of the librarians.

"Excuse me, is it possible to book one of the readers later today? I've got some research to do on old copies of the Herald."

"Yes, of course what time?"

"Three o'clock, the name's Matthew."

The librarian checked the system, entered Matt's details and advised him it was booked. Matthew thanked them, departed and walked straight back to his shop, forgetting to buy a coffee. He spent the next couple of hours at the shop with few customers coming in. He'd surfed the net in the hope of finding something but had failed to do so. At least he'd been able to close in on a possible time frame though, based on his own life events and his limited knowledge of Frank's activities. He'd hoped that Joe would have called in, after getting over his accusatory outcry, so he could pick his brains but he'd seen no sign of him. He'd call back when he was ready to, he always did.

Ten to three came and with no customers in, Matthew locked up the shop and headed off to the library. He remembered this time to grab a coffee and on entering the library, settled down at a reader, microfilms ready and began the laborious process. Two hours later he found it. April 1998. 'Tragic suicide of local woman at local railway station' the headline read. Matthew read through the article. That was when he recalled Anna Brown, she was in a relationship with Wellbury all those years ago. Another one of his many women and this lady had apparently killed herself. Appeals to locate a tramp in the area at the time, who may have been a witness, had identified nobody. The investigation brought up nothing and a coroner's hearing concluded that it was a suicide. The investigation was closed.

Matthew sat and pondered. A death, years ago of someone related to Wellbury, a tramp at the scene who was unidentified, now two murders in the town, one of them being Wellbury. Was there a connection here that the police were missing? He'd have to speak with Rachel; she was the expert and let's face it, the investigator that he wasn't. Anything to help though, he might have been right with the books.

He texted Rachel, who told him she'd be off work at seven. He could get home, go for a run and clear his head, shower and then come back for Rachel. He let her know his plans and left the library, copies of the newsprint in hand.

***

The Operation Torrent enquiry team had held their daily debrief, now Rachel was headed into the Operation Torrent management meeting. Boy, did the police service love meetings, they absolutely thrived on them, with many of them concluding that a further meeting was required, or a sub meeting, or a sub sub meeting. Rachel supposed that all large organisations were like this but still found it exasperating at times. However, today's meetings were required. Jones wanted action; he wanted the murderer in custody as soon as possible. They all did.

"To summarise ladies, gents," Jones started, "we have Marsden on bail for the Wellbury murder but he appeared to be at home for the Briggs one. Wilmslow is currently in hospital with uniformed guard, remains on bail, but we think she is more likely a witness than the offender. Greaves we now have under control, we have an image, we have his prints and DNA which are both at the labs. What else do we know about him, Andy?"

"He lives alone on the south side in a ground floor flat. He works as a hospital porter primarily at Fenchurch General but also does some bank work at Barnston. We know that he has a historic connection with Wellbury, whom we believe bullied him at school. We haven't yet worked out any connection with Briggs. Interestingly, he may also know Marsden, they were in the same school year. Surveillance are happy that they can control him and are booked for the next couple of days."

"Where are we with the prints and DNA?"

"Forensics have managed to get partial prints from the glass sir, not found in any crime scene yet. DNA is at the lab and is top priority for them," Rachel stated.

"Any friends at work, associates, someone he may confide in?"

"Not that we have found yet, boss," replied Andy.

"Keep looking," he addressed Andy, "I want this man in custody. We need to find a reason to bring him in. What about the trace drug found in Wellbury's blood profile? What is it? Is it something that you can get in a hospital? If this bloke is a porter, he may be able to get into anywhere in the hospital."

"It's identified as diachlorotine, a sedation drug. Hospitals do keep supplies of the drug."

"Let's see if there is any missing at Fenchurch or Barnston," continued Jones. "The plan going forward is full time surveillance on Greaves - if he does anything criminal, I want him lifted for it; Regular bail checks on Marsden; Wilmslow we will deal with when she is fit to be. This is the last push guys. We are nearly there. We just need a little more to bring him in, a little bit of luck." He checked his watch. "I need to go. Meeting finished. I'll see you all tomorrow."

***

Matt pulled up at the rear of the police station and sat waiting for two minutes before Rachel walked out and entered the car.

"Busy day love?" he asked.

"Very busy. How about you?"

"Ticking over at the shop, I've been busy doing some research too." Matthew drove steadily home where he parked up and they both entered the house.

"The fridge is bare," he said, "so we're on cheesy beans on toast."

"Mmm, comfort food," Rachel replied.

"So, you texted me today, about 'Coma'. What was that all about?"

"It's just something that's popped up in the investigation. It may be nothing. I've looked it up on the web, so it's all sorted."

"Good stuff. As I said, I've been doing some research myself today," continued Matthew, microwaving the beans. Matthew then recounted his findings at the library, producing the copied newspaper articles about Anna Brown's suicide.

"What do you think?"

"Well, it's old, old news Matt. The investigation was completed and no suspicious circumstances were found. The investigation file will probably be destroyed by now but there will be an electronic record of the details somewhere." Rachel smiled at Matthew, "You playing detective again? Why don't you just join the force and do it properly?" she joked.

"Me? No thanks. All that training, wearing a uniform, all the Sirs and Ma'ams. That's not me, Rach, it's more fun 'in the shadows'," responded Matt theatrically. "After all, you're my Lestrade." Rachel laughed.

"I hardly think so. You're more like a Clouseau." Matthew pretended to look crestfallen as he served up the beans.

"I've been thinking that we should do Fenchurch soon. It seems ages since we have been there."

"Sounds good, Matt. I'll get some time in the next couple of weeks. We could book a hotel, do the theatre and a meal if you like."

"Brilliant."

*** 

Rachel arrived at work at 7 am. The surveillance team would already be plotted at Greaves' home address, waiting for him to come out. Andy would be chasing the DNA screening today and Raheel's team were working hard on the Briggs investigation. She opened her email and had a confirmation email from the night sergeant that Marsden was at his mum's house when they bail checked him last night. Andy was going to make sure that he had one of the surveillance radios in his office today so that they could hear what was going on live.

She closed her emails and opened up the electronic intelligence system. The system held information on all persons who had ever had any dealings with the police as offenders, witnesses, victims of crime or where there was a specific reason to hold the information. The police couldn't just hold everything they ever received and so followed strict 'weeding' protocols whereby they had to delete data on persons if it was no longer required. Would Anna Brown's case file be retained on the system? There was only one way to find out, so Rachel entered her name. The system brought up a long list of different Anna Browns, as with any computer system, it was only as good as the people entering the data. Fortunately, it was hard to misspell Anna's name, however, Rachel would have to narrow down the search parameters. The easiest way was to try and cross reference with another person, providing that intelligence had linked them together. Rachel looked up Wellbury, checking his associate list for links to Anna, finding nothing. Stumped at the first hurdle, thought Rachel and cursed herself. "You stupid woman." She then brought the list of Anna's up again. The system would flag whether any of the Anna's was deceased and there on page two was 'Anna

Brown - deceased/suicide'. Rachel opened the record and began reading. The record held data about the case, such as witness statements of persons present at the station, the British Rail staff involved, family and medical accounts of Anna's wellbeing. Listed within, there was also a complaint against the police. Opening that document, Rachel determined that the family had been unhappy with the quality of the police investigation. Mr Brown had filed the complaint via his solicitor, who worked for a law firm in Barnston. The complaint had been photocopied and scanned onto the system. Rachel opened the document, which started;

*On behalf of my clients, Mr and Mrs D Brown, I, Sebastian Briggs, an associate of Watson Law Firm, make the following complaints against Barnston Police ...*

"What the hell!" exclaimed Rachel. She read the list of complaints which covered what the Browns believed was the incompetence of the police, but the important thing to Rachel was that Briggs was representing them. She had found a link between Wellbury and Briggs and the link was Anna Brown. *You are bloody brilliant, Matt*, she thought, reading on. So how could she progress this? She hated to open up old wounds but she could really do with speaking to the Browns. There was a landline for them on the system and provided that they hadn't moved addresses, she could make an appointment to see them. She jotted the number down and picked up the phone.

\*\*\*

"Hello, Donald Brown speaking."

"Mr Brown, my name is Detective Inspector Rachel Barnes of Barnston Police, there is nothing to worry about."

"Go on," Mr Brown replied suspiciously.

"I'd like to come and see you to see if you could help me tie up some loose ends I've got in a current investigation."

"Are you the lady that's been on the telly?"

"Yes, sir, that's me."

"Well, I don't know how I can help. I don't know anything about any of that."

"I know that you probably won't, Mr Brown, but if I could just have a chat, then it'll be done and I won't disturb you again."

"Very well officer, I'll be at home all day."

"Thank you, Mr Brown. I'll be at yours at eleven this morning." Rachel said goodbye and terminated the call.

***

Donald Brown placed down the phone receiver and turned to his wife.

"Lillian, it's the police, that woman from the television that's investigating those murders. She wants to come and see us. She's coming round at eleven this morning." Lillian looked flustered, smoothed her apron and reached into the front pocket for her mobile phone.

"Don't worry, dear," she said shakily, "I'll ring him." Lillian held her phone to her ear, sat down on the sofa and spoke.

"Hello, it's me. The police are coming to see us about the murders that have been on the TV. They think that we can help them. It's that detective woman off the television." She paused, listening and replied. "Eleven o'clock." She listened again and the call was terminated. She looked at her husband, stood up and took his hand, squeezing it. "Well, now he knows."

Richard put his phone down on the table. He had an extra shift at Barnston Hospital today so he'd need to get a move on. He switched off the television and jumped in the shower, thinking about the latest news. It looked like the local police had made no significant moves forward in the murder investigations. Briggs' wife and kids had been filmed returning to Barnston but couldn't stay at the family home so the police had put them at a safe, undisclosed location. No doubt the police would be trying to convince Mrs Briggs to do a press disclosure, asking the murderer to hand himself in. That female detective inspector hadn't been back on making any more ridiculous statements. He was sure that he had seen her around the town before but couldn't remember where. Having got dressed, he shoved some bits in his backpack and stepped out of his front door.

***

"All units: the subject has exited and locked his front door. He wears dark clothing and a dark backpack. Subject walks to a small outhouse which he unlocks with a key. Subject takes a black mountain bike out and re-locks the door. Subject and bike towards the gate and the street."

The surveillance team all prepared themselves. Two push bikes were taken out of cars and officers stood by them, waiting for directions. The team stood poised.

"Subject to the gate and is on the bike and left up the hill."

***

Richard stood up on his pedals, getting his bike going. The hill was fairly steep and would take him towards town where he wanted to grab something to eat to take to work. He checked behind him and saw a fat bloke with a beard cycling from the bottom of the hill in the same direction. *Good luck to him,* he thought, *he'd never make it up the hill and would probably have a heart attack trying.* Now with his momentum going, Richard sat and powered his way up towards traffic lights that had just turned amber. He checked quickly right and completed an 'ambler gambler', turning left around the corner. Behind him, and out of his view, the driver of a silver estate hit his steering wheel in frustration as he was held at the red light. Richard continued cycling, now freewheeling gently down the hill towards town. Pedestrians scuttled along the pavements doing daily chores and shopping. The weather was chilly but clear and bright and Richard was enjoying himself, oblivious that a surveillance team was following him. Ahead on the town road, an operative walked her dog, giving the subject's location and direction as he passed her. A car sat on the edge of town watched him cycle towards the precinct as the passenger got out on foot, ready to take up the follow. A fat bloke with a beard walked around the corner of the previous traffic lights, pushing a bike and taking in great gasps of air, exultant that he'd made the climb without collapsing. Richard came to a stop and walked into the town pushing his bike.

*\*\*\**

Joe walked out of his mother's house feeling horrendous and desperately needing to score some brown. He had no cash though so was going to need to generate some this morning. He was reluctant to head into town;

he couldn't be bothered speaking to anyone he knew. He'd been shoplifting there a bit too frequently and all the coppers in town would be looking out for him. He scanned around and saw nothing out of place. He'd have to assume that they could be following him at any time and set off, considering his route. He would use a few alleyways to wend his way through the estate, hold at a few places so he could see who was moving around.

Half an hour later, he was happy that the police were not following him. He'd seen nobody suspicious, no one twice and heard no cars tearing around the streets trying to find him. He now walked into the grounds of Barnston Hospital. He'd stolen from here before; it was amazing who may leave an office door open and what he may be able to pick up. If he was lucky, there would be a laptop or some phones lying around. He'd avoid iPads and iPhones as they may have 'find my pad/phone' activated. He put on his baseball cap and entered the hospital.

\*\*\*

Matthew had just sold a copy of 'Slinky Malinki' to a young mum who had been looking around the store with her young child. She had left with a smile on her face and her child seemed very happy with the bag he had been given to carry the book home in. He sipped on his coffee, going over in his head the discussions he'd had with Rachel about her investigation. She seemed confident that things were going in the right direction and he hoped that his additional input was helping her. He could never be a policeman but being part, albeit a very minor part, in a current police enquiry excited him. It was helping to fill in his mundane hours at work and he was feeling useful. He turned to his computer. Let's see how many Browns I have on my records, he thought, pushing the keys.

***

"Subject is back to his bike, having exited the bakery and is now walking right of the precinct towards the railway station." The town was busy with pedestrians. Greaves could be seen eating an item from a bakery bag as he walked. He stopped to check his bag and then continued. The operative had control and then heard a shout behind him. Two scruffy, drunken louts were shouting and pushing each other, a fight starting.

"Bloody idiots," said the operative, turning back towards Greaves.

"Damn," he said aloud, he was gone, disappeared, nowhere to be seen in the crowd.

"I've lost him," the operative transmitted over the airwaves.

***

Rachel walked out of the station, heading for town when her phone rang. Traffic was busy as she walked and talked.

"Yes, Andy."

"They've just lost him at the top of town."

"Not again! I'm there now, I'll take a look. What's he wearing?" Andy provided the details as Rachel scanned the area, cars speeding past her. About to cross, she hesitated. That car was coming too fast, it wasn't safe. Her peripheral vision caught a cyclist on the path. She tucked close to the kerb, to let them pass, concentrating on the approaching car.

Suddenly, a hard force hit her back and she fell forward. She screamed, brakes squealed, a sickening thud, bones broke as she was flung onto the bonnet of the vehicle. Pain, her head collided with the windscreen, blood streamed across her eyes then ... blackness.

Rachel lay in a mangled heap on the road, the driver of the vehicle hands to face and screaming. Blood streamed from Rachel's scalp, her right leg lay at an awkward angle, her face covered by tangled hair. Members of the public nearby got on their phones, calling for help, or ran in to help Rachel. Traffic was at a standstill. A uniformed copper walked out of the front of the police station and seeing the scene, immediately started to transmit on her radio as she ran towards the mess. Sirens sounded in the background. The cyclist continued on their route, now back on the road and headed towards Barnston Hospital.

***

Matthew interrogated the customer system, checking his watch and thinking he may nip out and get something to eat whilst he did the research. Over the past year he'd had five Browns order books from him. None of them may have any links at all to any of this; he'd have to take a look at the books that they had been ordering. He checked on one of the names when his phone rang. *Well, I never realised that*, he thought, looking at the screen as he answered.

"Hi, Matt speaking."

"Matthew, it's Andy from the police station, I work with Rachel. She's been in an accident, mate. The ambulance crew are with her now. Stay where you are and I'll send a car round to get you up to the hospital."

"What? Where? How did it happen?" Matthew sat shocked, hands starting to shake.

"I don't know but we'll get you up to the hospital and find out. We'll be there in five minutes. Wait at your shop. DO NOT drive."

The phone went dead and Matthew sat staring. *Rachel in an accident, getting treated... How bad was it? It would be bad if they were sending someone for him. In the middle of her investigation too, just when she was starting to make headway, this might take her off the case.* Matthew sat staring at the screen, not really paying attention to the name which stood flashing at him almost begging to be noticed. The doorbell to the shop sounded and a uniformed police officer walked in.

"Matthew?"

"Yes, that's me. The police car will be here shortly. I'll help you lock up and we can walk out together and get you up there." Matthew automatically went through shutting doors, turning lights off. He walked away from the counter to the door, turned the open sign to closed, locked the door and in a daze walked with the constable. On the counter, the computer database maintained its power, having not been switched off, displaying the last page that Matthew had been viewing, the name flashing its warning.

***

The ambulance crew had arrived at the scene and immediately the paramedics set to work. Her airway cleared, an oxygen mask was placed on Rachel as blood was wiped away from her face. Her eyes felt wet as the red film cleared and her head was banging. She was conscious again but struggling with the enormous pain on her right side. Green jumpsuits drifted in and out of view and she could hear her name called out distantly. Her body was moved by unseen hands as she felt the solidity of a stretcher encompass her. She didn't dare look down and never felt the prick of a needle as a Venflon was inserted to her left arm. She could fuzzily see a bag of water suspended above her, presuming they were fluids. She tried to talk, a groan coming out.

"It's OK Rachel. You're in safe hands. We're going to be heading to the hospital."

The sky moved above her as she felt her body lifted and her view was replaced by the inside of an ambulance. Head held rigid by a strap, she groaned again.

"A little something for the pain," she heard as it eased slightly. "That'll be enough to get you through the journey, then we'll assess it in A and E." Rachel felt the ambulance move as sirens were switched on and she drifted.

***

Matthew climbed into the police car, his numbness receding, replaced by a new sense of urgency. He needed to get to Rachel, to speak to her, to check that she was OK. His mind spinning with images of Rachel lying on the road, crying out in pain, ambulance and police lights flashing around her. Flashing 'On/Off', 'On/Off', his brain in overdrive, flashing 'On/Off', 'On/Off'. He grabbed his hair frantically, cradling his brain, trying to grasp and control the image. *The lights,* he thought, *those bloody lights.* Flashing, flashing like his screen cursor, flashing a name. *He had to get to Rachel, to tell her.*

"We'll get you up there safely, sir. Rachel is conscious and she's on her way to A and E. Everything will be OK. Belt on please."

Matthew complied as the car drove steadily away, heading for the hospital.

# Chapter 17

Joe watched the door that led from the staff changing area at the hospital. It was usually locked but now and again someone would forget to close it properly, which would give Joe the opportunity to enter and have a rake around. He'd grab some uniform when he got in and if challenged, he could pretend that he was getting changed from work, throw them in a gurney and leave with no one the wiser. He'd been there only a couple of minutes when a bloke in theatre blues walked out, adjusted his glasses and headed off down the corridor.

*Hang on a minute, wasn't that Greaves that he used to go to school with?* He looked familiar and Joe was sure that he'd seen him in Forseti's bookshop before. His interest piqued, Joe followed Greaves down the corridor to see where he ended up going. Greaves walked at a brisk pace and Joe just caught him turning left towards A and E. He followed discreetly and waited at the closed doorway, looking through the glass.

"You OK, sir?" said a female voice. Joe turned around to see a lady wearing a physio uniform.

"Oh, yes," he replied "I'm fine. Just waiting for a friend of mine who has nipped in there."

"OK," said the physio, pushing against the door and entering.

*\*\*\**

Richard walked into Accident and Emergency, his theatre blues sticking to him, following his ride into work. He'd been a little late so had to push it and once changed, headed to the department. Walking through waiting patients, he headed to the emergency entrance where an ambulance was pulling in. A nurse stood waiting.

"You there, grab that trolley. We'll get her straight on to one of ours and get her in for assessment." Richard did as instructed: grabbed the trolley and took it to the rear of the ambulance. The doors opened and a crew man stepped out, holding the stretcher end.

"One, two, three and ... lift." The nurse stepped up to the head end of the trolley.

"Rachel, you've arrived at Barnston Accident and Emergency. I'm Linda. We'll get you sorted."

Rachel attempted to smile through her oxygen mask but couldn't move the rest of her body as she was strapped down to prevent further injury. She tried to say something but heard "Don't try to talk. We'll get all this sorted when we are inside." The nurse nodded and a blue clad figure loomed over Rachel preparing to push the trolley. She looked straight up to his face and looked straight into the eyes of Richard Greaves, who smiled down at her. She tried to move but couldn't. Tried to shout, but only a loud groan came out. Eyes wide open, pulse racing, she was terrified. Her suspect killer was here.

"Now, now, Rachel. Everything is going to be alright. You're in safe hands now." He beamed at her and pushed her into the hospital.

Her mind raced as her lungs gasped for breath, the beeping noise of her pulse increasing through the heart monitor. Head pounding, she struggled to focus on the face above her. She attempted to move but was held fast by secure strapping. *Don't let him near me, don't let him near me,* she screamed inside her head, helpless and incapacitated. *He's a bloody murderer* ... she sank into unconsciousness, her mind overwhelmed by her situation.

\*\*\*

Joe looked through the window and saw Greaves and a nurse pushing a woman on a trolley into a cubicle. A minute later, a male in blue scrubs, with a stethoscope around his neck entered the same cubicle. The nurse walked towards the nurses' station and Greaves stood outside the curtained area, hands clasping nervously.

\*\*\*

Stirring, Rachel had seen Greaves leave and relaxed. So, he bloody worked in Accident and Emergency. She needed help; surely one of her colleagues would arrive soon. A second gentle faced older male had entered and looking down at her, gave a friendly smile.

"Hello Rachel, I'm Dr Geoffrey Brown, consultant anaesthetist and am here to assess your suitability for surgery." Rachel looked at his face, then his name badge 'Dr Geoff Brown' written thereon, a red stethoscope dangling around his neck.

"Now, I've brought a little something to give you to help you relax," he produced a small syringe and pushed the air from it, inserting it into the Venflon lead and pushing the contents in. "Now, your mouth may feel a bit dry, I believe that Mr Wellbury's will have." Rachel looked at him. *Did he just say Mr Wellbury?*

"Also, it will affect your speech. Just dull your vocal cords a little," he smiled. Rachel felt her throat tighten and her mouth dry, she gave a weak whimper. "I'm sorry to do this to you, detective, but you see, you were getting too close. I'd finished what needed doing but you kept prodding, kept poking, determined to get me. You rang my brother and his wife. They don't need to be dragged

219

into this; it was my choice."

"Everything OK?" the nurse's head poked through the curtain.

"All fine, thanks Linda. Rachel will be going straight into theatre soon."

The curtain closed leaving a small gap. Richard outside, moved closer, listening.

"So, you'll be going to the theatre in a few minutes. I'll be your anaesthetist. Have you heard of the book 'Coma'?" Rachel struggled. "It'll be a tragic accident, death by natural causes. No one needs to know anything else. After all, that was the conclusion with my niece Anna. You bloody lot couldn't care less. You don't care that an innocent young lady died prematurely. It ripped our family apart. No justice. Well now there is. All tied up neatly. Wellbury, Briggs, and now young Greaves to blame for it."

\*\*\*

A marked police car pulled up directly outside A and E and a police officer exited, opening the rear passenger door. The door shoved forcefully back as Matthew leapt from the car heading into the hospital. The officer followed at pace. Matthew headed for the reception desk where a surly looking lady looked at him and forced a smile.

"Can I help you sir?" she asked politely.

"I'm looking for Rachel Barnes. She's just been brought in. A police officer. Road accident," he sputtered out.

"Oh yes," she stated, noting the uniformed officer behind Matthew. "She's in cubicle 7 and…" Looking left she spotted Linda and added, "being looked after by

Linda," as she indicated to the nurse approaching the station. Matthew turned to her.

"How's Rachel? I'm her partner. I need to see her."

"She's stable, sir. I've just left her and the anaesthetist is looking after her."

"I need to see her," he repeated, looking over her head towards the patient cubicles. He looked away then down to Linda. His head snapped back to the cubicles.

"Wait a minute, is that Greaves?" he said in disbelief.

Pushing Linda to one side he moved, walking past her, pace increasing, running.

***

Richard looked right then left, *what should he do? This man was insane.* There was a yell in the corridor. He looked right to see Matthew Forster running at him, a police officer behind.

"Get away from her!" screamed Matthew in a rabid frenzy, barging Richard aside and

pulling back curtains.

***

Through the glass, Joe saw Matt run at Greaves and barge him. Joe pushed through the door and ran to help, grabbing an empty metal bedpan as he did. Greaves shouted, "It's him, it's him!" pointing into the cubicle as he fell backwards.

"You!" Matthew stood dumbstruck. Stood next to the trolley was Geoff from the bookshop, syringe in hand, preparing to administer another dose. Matthew leapt in, tried to grab Geoff, but was pushed back. Geoff stood, needle extended threateningly.

"You'll get this. It'll kill you!" he screamed, stepping out of the cubicle and backing down the corridor. "Stay back."

"It's him. He's the murderer!" screamed Greaves excitedly, pointing at Geoff.

Matt looked to Rachel, who remained strapped down, then surreally, saw Joe creeping up behind Brown, metal bedpan in hand. Joe's arm drew back and swung forward, the bedpan colliding with Brown's head. Brown dropped like a sack of potatoes, syringe clattering to the side. Of all the people, Greaves then dived on top of Brown, holding him down. The uniformed police officer and his driver came running through, calling on the radio for assistance. They looked at each other, not knowing where to start. Matthew moved to Rachel protectively. He looked at the cops and gestured.

"Him and him," he pointed to Geoff and Richard. *He had no idea what was happening but Joe was already under arrest for the murders so they may as well take the other two.* The officers looked at each other and cuffed them both, protestations coming from Richard Greaves' mouth. They'd sort this out at the station. More officers entered the area.

"Right. Enough!" bellowed a female voice. "Get out of my way, this lady needs surgery!" shouted Linda. Porters in blues took either end of the trolley, allowed Matthew to give Rachel a kiss, and wheeled her out in the direction of the theatre. Linda looked at Matthew. "She'll be out for a couple of hours. Let's get some details from you and I'll make sure that you see her as soon as you can." Matthew squeezed Joe's shoulder gratefully and walked away with the nurse.

"Joe Marsden, if you can come with us, please. We'll need to get some details from you and work out what the hell's been going on," the police officer said. Joe smiled at Matt.

"See you soon" Joe said, then walked away, for once willingly, with a uniformed police constable.

## May 2016

Matthew sat in Forseti's, staring at his full bookshelves which were in immaculate order, in the way that he liked. The door to the shop opened and he turned to see Joe striding in with a smile on his face.

"Good morning my son, how are you on this beautiful day?"

"Fine thanks Joe, fine." Matthew looked outside, where the sun was beaming down on an unusually mild May day.

He held up his full coffee cup. "Do you want one?"

"Don't mind if I do," replied Joe, taking the cup from Matthew's hands. "How's Rach?"

"She's doing OK, still recovering. Going slightly mad at home but building up her strength. She's going to take a career break."

"To do what?"

"No idea. Just away from the police. The investigation and accident have taken a lot out of her. She's done her bit for now and needs to recharge. Brown's away, hopefully for good. Greaves is a star witness and probably revelling in it and you, my friend, are a free man."

"I know, and it feels great. I'm on a withdrawal programme and am gonna try and stick to it. It's ruined my life and I need to rebuild."

"That's good to hear. Rachel and I are going to go away for a while. I've got an old uni friend who is going to come in and manage the shop. He's gonna need a hand from someone local. You fancy the job?"

Joe stood there astounded. "You'd do that for me?"

"The man who saved Rach's life with a metal bedpan! How could I not?"

"You're on. I'd love to. Thank you so much for believing in me."

Joe and Matt sat talking about the details before Joe got up to go. He opened the door to leave and turned to Matt, "I didn't ask, Matt. Where are you going to go?"

"We're off to Scotland, mate. I've always had a hankering for living there. Rach and I are going to take a look around and see what life throws at us."

The door to Forseti's closed for the time being as Matthew picked up his phone to ring Rachel and tell her the good news.

## Acknowledgements

Thank you to Claire Voet and the team at Blossom Spring Publishing for supporting me with my debut novel.

Thanks to my children, my sister and my wonderful wife for all of your tolerance, support and positivity, "If you never try, you'll never know."

www.blossomspringpublishing.com

Printed in Great Britain
by Amazon

20274400R00133